REDEMPTION

A Love's Valley Historical Romance

REDEMPTION

•

Carolyn Brown

AVALON BOOKS
NEW YORK

Brown

Published by Thomas Bouregy & Co., Inc.
160 Madison Avenue, New York, NY 10016

Library of Congress Cataloging-in-Publication Data

Brown, Carolyn, 1948–
Redemption / Carolyn Brown.
p. cm.
ISBN 0-8034-9766-0 (alk. paper)
I. Title.

PS3552.R685275R45 2006
813'.54—dc22
2005034690

PRINTED IN THE UNITED STATES OF AMERICA
ON ACID-FREE PAPER
BY HADDON CRAFTSMEN, BLOOMSBURG, PENNSYLVANIA

21.95
7/12/04

b12437682 DA

For Bill and Marge Brown

Chapter One

A daddy longlegs spider dropped from the cellar wall onto Geneva's bare arm. Fearful as she was of any kind of spider, she willed herself to not scream as a shudder shook her so hard it was a miracle the evil men decked out in white sheets with white hoods over their heads didn't hear her bones rattling together. If they found her, she would without a doubt soon be dead.

Using his long spindly legs, the spider traveled up her arm, across her chest and down the other arm. Still she kept her silence even in the wake of all the fuss going on out in the yard. They'd ridden up on their horses, white robes billowing behind them in the summer breeze like clouds being tossed around by the wind. When Hiriam had stepped out on the porch, they'd grabbed him and began yelling something about him being unfit to be a Southern man.

Geneva had been gathering green apples in the orchard and the sight of those ghostly apparitions had scared her so much that she'd hidden behind the well house, peeping around the corner to watch the intruders search the house, the basement, and even the attic. When they were satisfied that no one else was around, they'd begun to question Hiriam.

"Where is your worthless wife? We have had report that she was seen giving help to the wife of the man we strung up last week for looking at a white woman the wrong way down near the general store. We heard she went right into the widow's home and served those people. That ain't the kind of thing your wife should be doing," one shouted.

"She's in the house, making an apple pie," Hiriam said. "I beat her soundly when I found that she'd done such a deed. Gave her ten lashes with the buckle end of my belt. Y'all know I wouldn't tolerate such outlandish behavior."

"That's not good enough and I think you are lying, Hiriam. You wouldn't have the guts to beat anyone— not even a woman—with the buckle end of a belt. You should've known better than to bring home one of those tinker people, Hiriam. If we can't have her, we'll hang you, so you'd better tell us where she is, or we'll find her. You know we will and she's going to pay for what she's done. Can't have other white women acting like that. We'll have to make an example out of her," he said.

"I swear, she was in the kitchen when you rode up. Making pie crust. Believe me, you won't have to take care of her. I will. I promise. You've got my word on it. I'll kill her myself. You can watch," he said seriously, beads of sweat popping out on his forehead and running down his flabby cheeks in streams.

"Hiriam, Hiriam," the man chuckled. "You should know better than to take a wife of the tinkers, even if you did win her in a game of cards. You could have just used her and then left her, but to bring home such a woman to grace the plantation your father worked his whole life to build . . . that alone should be a hanging offense, but to bring home one who'd take the side of the slaves against you, that's definitely a hanging offense. It's not even natural for her to be down there in that part of town, serving food up to them men folks. You knew better than to allow it. We warned you she was spending too much time with the likes of them. She's not in the house, or in the outhouse. We searched. Why do you protect her?" The man grabbed a rope, deftly tied the knots, and shook the noose at Hiriam.

"Protect her!" Hiriam shouted, his voice hoarse with fear. "I'm sorry I ever went up to that part of the country. I'm sure enough sorry I let that old man use her for money. Turn me loose and I'll even help you find her. Check the orchard. Maybe she went there for more apples. I'll put the noose around her sorry neck myself."

The man jerked his head in the direction of the orchard and three others started in that direction. Before they had rounded the end of the house, Geneva had slipped down into the basement. She'd wanted to shut the wooden doors behind her, close out all the sunlight and hide in the darkness until they were gone. But something reminded her that they might notice the doors were shut when they'd been open before. Hiriam was going to be mad when they finally let him go, but he wouldn't hit her again. Not ever. She'd vowed that the last night he'd slapped her across the face for helping Mazell after those wicked men hung her husband from a tree in the cemetery. The fact that he was alive testified to the fact that he'd never hit her with the buckle end of a belt. And if he thought he was going to shoot her or hang her, he'd better think again.

She tried to make herself smaller by huddling into a back corner, waiting, hoping they wouldn't find her. Hiriam wouldn't care if they did hang her. He'd said a year ago that as soon as she produced a male heir, he intended to get rid of her. She could go back to the tinkers or down to Mazell's for all he cared. To him she was nothing more than a brood mare. One Garner male to carry on the plantation—that's all he wanted.

"Ain't nobody in the orchard," the two men reported back to their boss.

"Hiriam, did you lie to us?" the biggest one chuckled.

"I did not. You are my best friends. I ride with you. Wear the robes and cover my face just like you do," Hiriam said. "Geneva, wherever you are, come out here right now and tell these men you've been punished for your wicked deeds," he yelled back toward the house.

The big man slipped the noose around Hiriam's neck and led him like a puppy dog to the ancient pecan tree at the back of the house. He tossed the end over a limb twice and knotted it, tested it to be sure the knot would hold and nodded at the other men. They lifted Hiriam up into the saddle of one of their horses.

"Now one more time. Where is she hiding?" the man asked.

"For the love of God, man, I don't know where she is but you've got my word on it, I'll deliver her to you the minute I find her. You think I'd die for a tinker's daughter that I won in a card game. Man, I wouldn't have even married her but I been lookin' for a wife ever since the war ended and there she was. Besides I wanted a son to leave my plantation to. One who'd carry on the family traditions," Hiriam whined.

"That's not acceptable," he said. "Not at all, Hiriam."

Very gently, he picked up the reins of the horse and urged him forward until the rope was taunt. "Got anything more to say?" he asked.

"I told you all I know," Hiriam gasped.

Then the horse walked right out from under Hiriam. He grabbed at the rope around his neck and uttered a hoarse scream but the rope held tight and the strong tree limb scarcely even wobbled. His body danced awhile, jerking and shivering as he died.

It was as if Geneva was lost in a dream, the spider returning to walk across her arms and around her legs as she sat on the dirt floor and tried to still the rapid beating of her heart as she watched her husband hang. Even if he was a worthless man and an even more despicable husband, he was human and she should feel something for him. But it wasn't there in the numbness she'd known for the past year, since the middle of the night when her drunken father awoke her from a deep sleep and told her she was going to marry the man he'd been playing cards with all that day and into the night.

"Burn the house to the ground. If she comes home from that slave's place then by damn, she won't have a place to live in. We'll find her. If not today, then tomorrow," the man said.

Geneva stuffed her fist into her mouth and tried to curl up in a tighter ball. The sickening smell of kerosene filtered through the kitchen floorboards right above her head. Smoke oozed down between the cracks. She wrapped the tail of her apron up over her nose and waited until she heard the hooves of their horses and shouts as the men rode away. Then she stood up, found the jar where she'd seen Hiriam hide money behind the rack of canned apples, and twisted the lid open. Shoving the money into her pocket and stomping the spider attempting to run away from the smoke and heat at the same time, she ran out to the orchard and slid down the rough bark of a tree, still shaking, wondering if she was dreaming.

She pinched herself on the arm to check that she was really awake. Flames engulfed the house, the lovely curtains billowing out the windows with the wind of the heat. She fingered the money in her pocket. What to do? Where to go? She had to make some quick decisions. No one could help her except Mazell and they'd be watching her house. She took a deep breath, stiffened her spine and took one long, last look at the house she had never been welcome in. A marriage that was nothing but a farce. A man who'd never loved her or even cared if she lived or died. A waste of a year of her life.

She turned her back on it and with the first step began a long journey. First things first, she had to get out of Savannah. Out of Georgia. Back to the Carolinas or even beyond. As far as the money in her pocket would take her. Hopefully the men in the white sheets would be celebrating their victory over Hiriam until later tonight and by then she'd be on the first stagecoach out of town, as long as it would take to get back up north, back into territory she was vaguely familiar with.

Three miles later, just before lunchtime, she reached the stage station. "When does the next stage leave and where is it going?" she asked in a hollow voice.

"Next one leaves in ten minutes. Going thirty miles up the road into South Carolina to Ridgeland. All-nighter, it is. You want a ticket? What happened to you?" the station manager asked.

"Nothing. I'm just leaving town," she said shoving two bills on the counter.

"I'll make change," he said. "You'll get there in the morning by breakfast time, lady. Don't I know you?"

"No, you surely do not. Keep the change," she said.

"Yes, ma'am, never seen you before in my life," he

grinned. "Like I said, stage will be leaving from right there in ten minutes." He pointed toward a bench against the wall. Geneva drew her bonnet up over her head and waited. It was the longest ten minutes she'd ever spent in her life.

Harry Reed Hamilton whistled as he rode in the back of a Savannah taxi that lovely summer morning. It was the last day of June. Seemed symbolic somehow that he'd leave Georgia at the end of the month and begin a new one on his journey back home to Love's Valley, Pennsylvania. His commitment had finally finished. He'd agreed to a year posing as a soldier helping with the construction and it had stretched to more than two years. He had a few papers in his trunk to deliver to the President of the United States in Washington, D. C., and then he declared he wasn't leaving Love's Valley for a decade. Maybe even longer.

He'd be the only Hamilton brother to come home without a wife or a story behind it, and that was fine. His sister, Indigo, who hated all things Southern would be so proud of him. A brother who finally arrived in the valley without Rebel baggage. His oldest brother, Herman Monroe, had been on his way home when he found a Texas lady sitting on her trunk in the middle of the road. From the letters he'd received, the Texan was fitting in right well with the family despite Indigo's sharp tongue. The middle brother, Henry Rueben, had suffered a bit of amnesia and wound up with a Louisiana bayou woman. Reed had met her a few months earlier as they traveled home to Love's Valley. Lovely lady. Just what old Rueben needed. But a Southern wife wasn't for Reed. He'd be the brother who settled into Love's Valley a few years before he went looking for a wife. The youngest of the three brothers and only five years older than Indigo, he had plenty of time.

"Can't imagine, if you're going to Washington D. C., why you don't just get on a ship. Be a lot faster and more comfortable," the taxi driver said as he unloaded Reed's trunk in front of the stage station.

"Faster but not more comfortable. I suffer from sea sickness just looking at a fishing boat. Can't imagine staying on one of those things for a couple of weeks. Give me a stagecoach with all its bouncing around any day. At least I know I can put one foot on dry ground at any time," Reed handed the driver the fare.

"Well good luck to you and safe journey home," the driver smiled.

"Thank you. I'm sure it will be a long, boring journey, but that's fine by me," Reed said with a wave of his hand as he walked up to the small window where tickets were bought. "Next stage leaves when?" he asked.

"Five minutes. Going up to Ridgeland. An all-nighter. Ain't much between here and there but Hardeeville and that's too close to call it a day. Besides there's a big shipment on the stage and it's got to get to Ridgeland by morning," he said.

"From there where does the line go?" Reed asked.

"To Walterboro. Takes a couple of days but there's

a stage station in between with a couple of rooms to let and half decent food, I'm told," he said.

"Then give me fare to Ridgeland," Reed said.

"Where's the final destination?" the man asked.

"Love's Valley, Pennsylvania," Reed smiled.

"Long way," the man handed him a ticket and made change from the money Reed handed him. "Only got one other passenger. Woman out there." He pointed toward a fat woman wearing a dirty dress and even dirtier bonnet sitting on the bench.

"Thank you," Reed said, working hard not to snarl his nose at the woman. She looked as if she'd smell if he got too close and yet there would be no way to get away from her in the stage. Suddenly his perfect day had a flaw in it and his lighthearted mood weighed heavy on his heart. He just hoped she wasn't one of those big old women who wanted to talk nonstop all night long.

He leaned on a porch post and watched the stage rumble down the street. Nothing unusual. A driver. A shotgun rider. Both looked to be about his age. In less than ten minutes they'd unloaded a couple of trunks belonging to a newly married couple by the way the stars still hung around them and their smiles.

"No passengers!" He heard the driver arguing with the station manager. "The load is too dangerous to take on passengers with it."

"Those aren't my instructions," the little man puffed out his chest and pushed his eyeglasses back up on his sweaty nose. "No one told me there couldn't be passengers and I've booked that woman and man to go to Ridgeland. You'll be rid of them come morning light and if you don't want to haul passengers with your payload then you should've said so before I sold them tickets. Right now you're going to take that man and woman with you. Good Lord, man, you got a shotgun rider if trouble presents itself."

"Don't say you wasn't warned," the driver said. "People come back on you if something happens. You just remember it wasn't my idea to take on passengers with what we're haulin'."

"I'll remember," the little man grinned.

"Load 'em up. What kind of baggage you got?" The driver's nose wrinkled at the smoky, nasty smell of the big woman on the bench.

"Just what you see," Geneva stood up and started toward the stage.

"One trunk," Reed pointed toward the baggage on the wooden sidewalk.

Reed had been raised a gentleman so in spite of the way he felt about the fat, dirty woman, he held the door of the stage open for her. She barely nodded in thanks and kept her eyes on the station where four men stomped down the wooden sidewalk to the station window.

"Looking for Mrs. Hiriam Garner," the one who'd been the ringleader of those behind the lynching leaned against the window, a bright star pinned to his vest.

"What's she look like?" the station manager asked.

"Good lookin' woman. Blond hair. Big blue eyes. Hiram said she might be in town today," he said.

"Ain't seen a soul like that," the station manager told him honestly.

"Told you she wouldn't be in town. Bet those ex-slaves are hiding her out, but they can't hide a looker like her forever. She'll have to surface sometime," one of the others said.

Geneva pulled her bonnet down farther over her eyes and kept them downcast so no one could see their color. She could have reached out and touched any one of the four of them. Could have taken the knife from her pocket and slashed at least two throats before they even knew what hit them, but who'd believe those four were wearing white sheets and hanging Hiriam not two hours ago? Not the sheriff, two deputies and the mayor of Savannah, Georgia.

Reed stepped into the carriage and slid across the opposite seat from the woman, keeping as much distance as the tiny interior of a coach allowed. She reeked of smoke and filth. Her faded dress was tattered around the bottom. Lace on the tail of her petticoat hung in shreds. The toes of her boots were scuffed and worn almost through. Curiosity, it's said, is what killed the cat. It might not have killed Reed but it sure had his overactive imagination galloping ahead. Evidence was written all over the big woman that she was running away from something. She still wore her apron. Her face and hands were smutty with smoke and dirt.

"Name is Reed Hamilton," he said after the coach had gotten underway.

She nodded but offered nothing.

He'd been afraid she'd talk his ears plumb off through the night. It certainly appeared he was going to make it to Ridgeland with both ears intact if a brief nod was all she would do.

He could hear her stomach growling by the time they stopped at Hardeeville for supper. The station manager had a pot of passable beef stew and corn-bread made that morning. The woman took her meal in the farthest corner of the small dining room. The stage driver and shotgun rider ate together, both sullen and barely speaking through the meal. Reed hoped the more than eight-hundred-mile trip, which he figured would easily take five weeks, wouldn't be as tension filled as it had been the first ten miles, and he sure enough hoped the fat lady would be staying in Ridgeland.

"You two sure you want to ride all night? There's another stage coming through here in the morning. You could stay here, get a good night's rest and not have to sleep sitting up in a coach," the driver suggested, his voice edgy.

"I'd just as soon go on," Reed said, a prickly sensation tickling the nape of his neck. Something absolutely wasn't right and it had been his job the past two years to investigate things that weren't right.

"Lady?" the driver nodded toward her. "Plain you and the Mister here is at cross horns. Can't blame you none. There he is all dressed fit for Sunday dinner with the President himself and you in nothing but rags, but you don't have to stay with him, you know. You could stay right here and catch another stage."

"I'll go," she said, not bothering to explain that she wasn't with the man or wasn't likely to be with another man ever. Let them think what they would. Geneva didn't care, but she did want to be farther away from Savannah than ten miles in case that station manager decided to remember that he'd seen her a year ago when she got off the stage with Hiriam as his new bride.

"Have it your way. Just don't whine," the driver gritted his teeth.

Sometime after midnight, Geneva's chin dropped down on her chest and she fell asleep only to dream of spiders, fires, and lynchings. The stage rocked along, hitting a pothole and jarring her awake. The man who'd said his name was Reed Hamilton didn't seem to stir no matter how rough the road. He'd positioned his head in the corner of the stage and slept like only innocent children are capable of doing. Geneva stared at him. Dark brown hair cut above his ears. Black lashes resting on his cheeks. Eyes the color of pecan shells. Light brown with darker flecks she'd noticed earlier when he was looking out the window and wasn't watching her. An angular face that would make most women take a second look and then probably blush behind their fan. Not a spare ounce of flesh on his tall frame, just hard muscles in his arms and legs that stretched the fabric of his clothing. A handsome man to be sure, but she wasn't one bit interested in any kind of man. Handsome. Ugly. One with horns or a halo. They were all just alike when push came to shove: worthless.

Following his example, she leaned into the far corner of the stage and wiggled until she was semicomfortable and went back to sleep . . . one more time.

Chapter Two

Reed awoke with a start when the rhythm of the stage came to an abrupt halt. He pulled back the curtain over the window to a full lover's moon shining in the bed of a million twinkling stars. A gentle night breeze flowed through the window and he inhaled deeply, wondering why they'd stopped in the middle of the night. Even the refreshing night air couldn't dispel the odor inside the stage though. He could still smell the sleeping woman—a strange mixture of smoke, dirt and something else . . . the sweat of fear. It was unmistakable. He'd experienced the odor too many times in the war and he'd recognize it anywhere. But what did the woman have to fear and why hadn't he realized she was afraid of something or someone before now? With her height and girth she could probably whip any man on either side of the Mason-Dixon Line.

16

The business end of a rifle snaked through the window before he could collect his thoughts. Were they being robbed? He hadn't heard a single gunshot or any loud voices, but the rifle sure didn't look friendly and the noise of the hammer being cocked back didn't leave much doubt that whoever was on the other end wasn't playing games.

"What do you want?" he asked cautiously, fighting the desire to jerk his hidden pistol from the holster under his jacket and fire randomly out the window.

"We want you and your missus to step out of the stage right easy like. You shoulda stayed back there like we asked you," the driver's voice let him at least know who was holding the rifle. He started to tell the man that the big, dirty woman wasn't his missus but before he could open his mouth, she awoke with a stifled scream and tried to disappear into the corner of the stage.

"I said for the both of you to get on out here," the driver said again. "And I mean right now, not sometime tomorrow mornin' after breakfast."

Reed stepped out and held the door for the woman who appeared to have trouble breathing. That's all he needed—for the woman to faint. Fat as she was, it would take all six of the horses pulling the stage to get her back on her feet. "What is this all about and why do you have a gun trained on me?" he asked.

"We tried to get you to stay in the station, but you wouldn't have none of it. So now you can just be stranded out here. Shorty's already tossed your trunk off in the road. Hope there ain't nothing in it that'll break," he grinned. "We're robbing this stage, you see. There's a big shipment of money and it's going with us. Trouble is, you ain't goin' with us. Reckon it's at least ten or fifteen miles to Ridgeland. You're a settin' right in the middle of the best cotton land in the whole United States. Trouble is there ain't no slaves left to work the land. Just a bunch of burned out plantation homes. So don't be thinkin' you'll get to a town and report all this anytime right soon. Find you a bunch of slave quarters and settle down for a spell. Never know, you might even make up from whatever it is you're fightin' about. I got me a feelin' it's because you're so selfish you won't even buy your woman a decent dress. Take a big one to fit over all that woman but you could keep her outfitted decent, man. Anyway, you can fight or make up. Don't be makin' me no never mind since you got nowhere to go and a long time to get there," the man said with a chuckle as he jumped back up onto the stage.

The horses took off with a start when the driver cracked the whip over their heads. Reed retrieved his pistol from a shoulder strap under his jacket and took careful aim but didn't fire. If they returned fire with their rifles, they would have to be poor shots not to hit him or the woman. He didn't need either one. Not a gunshot wound for himself out in the middle of nowhere. Nor one for the woman. Lord, he could just imagine trying to carry someone that big to find help. His back would be broken in less than a mile and the stage driver had said it was a long way to town. He put the gun back and sat down on the trunk which had miraculously landed upright.

Bewildered. That's what he felt. He'd been awakened out of a deep sleep, tossed out beside the road like undesirable trash, and most likely that woman's relatives were going to be hotter than blue blazes when they found out she'd spent the night with him unchaperoned. But he'd be sold down the river as a slave and spend the rest of his days in the South, fighting prejudice and monster-sized mosquitoes before he did the honorable thing and made an honest woman out of her. It might not be her fault she was as big as the broad side of a barn. But it sure wasn't his that they were sitting in the middle of little more than a cattle trail where in all likelihood no stage would ever come by, nor people either.

Geneva didn't even know she was holding her breath until it came out in a great gush when she realized that the men with the guns weren't wearing flapping white robes. She didn't care if they were robbing the stage. All she hoped was that she was far enough away from Savannah that the sheriff and his cohorts didn't come looking for her. She melted in a heap, leaning back against the trunk Reed sat on. He'd drawn a pistol so fast it seemed like pure magic but he hadn't used it even after he'd taken a fierce stance and pointed it toward the stage. A sudden rage filled her breast. Anger for everything that had happened in the past twenty-four hours.

"Why didn't you shoot those sorry scoundrels?" she demanded in a frosty tone.

"It would have only angered them," he said. "Then they would have shot back and no doubt we'd be a couple of dead carcasses lying in the middle of the road right now. You got to know when to hold 'em and when to fold 'em."

"And I suppose you are a gambler too?" Her tone was even more icy than before.

"No, just a soldier going home," he said.

"Union?" she asked.

"That's right," he said.

She set her jaw and didn't say another word. She had nothing to say to those who'd fought in the War of Northern Aggression. They'd ruined a total way of life. Not that the Tuatha'an, the traveling people, or tinkers as most people called them, had any land to defend or worry about. The only dirt they owned was what stuck to their shoes or their wagon wheels. But she'd done business with the Southern people in South Carolina, Georgia, North Carolina and Virginia all her life and she hated what the war had done to the gracious way they'd lived. Not that Geneva had any truck with those who owned other people, either. No one ought to be owned by another being. She'd sure enough walked a mile in a slave's shoes the past year. Being married to Hiriam was the same as being owned by him, maybe even worse. A slave could at least escape to their quarters come nightfall. Living with Hiriam had been a twenty-four hour nightmare.

Reed slipped off the trunk and leaned against the

other end. "Guess we might as well sleep away what's left of the night. When daybreak comes we'll find a way out of here, hopefully," he said.

She didn't answer. She didn't need a Union soldier to get her to the nearest town and she still had enough money hidden in her pocket to buy a stage ticket farther north. If she didn't find the traveling people and rejoin them, there was always the possibility her mother's sister, Aunt Minnie, in Lynchburg, Virginia, would take her in for a few months. Aunt Minnie had thrown a fit when her mother fell in love with one of the Tuatha'an, so the story went. But maybe she'd have a soft spot after all these years for the daughter that union produced.

Sleep finally weighed her eyelids down until they shut out the moon and stars and even the plans of going to Virginia. But they didn't slam the door on the terrible dreams of men in white chasing her through the apple orchard, a noose shaking in the sheriff's hand and evil pouring from all their eyes, the only thing visible through the hoods over their heads.

"Well, what we got here?" a deep voice awoke both Reed and Geneva.

Reed grabbed for his gun.

Geneva jumped, her feet trying to run even though she was sitting on the ground.

"Don't reckon you'd be needin' that pistol, mister," the huge woman laughed. "Less'n you be one of them Klan men that goes about killin' and murderin' the old slaves in the countryside."

Reed took his hand from the pistol and Geneva got

control of the urge to tear out through the swamp like a scared rabbit. The big black woman reminded her of Mazell, only even larger than her friend back in Savannah, and maybe twenty years older. She was the color of coal and had at least three chins, all of them jiggling as she laughed at Reed and Geneva.

"Now what would a white couple be doin' a settin' in the middle of the road with a big ole travelin' trunk between them?" she asked.

"We were on our way to Ridgeland," Geneva said. "The stage driver and his shotgun rider decided to rob the stage and they threw us off right here. Said it was miles and miles into a town of any size."

"I reckon he'd be right about that," the woman nodded, pursing her full lips together seriously. "I reckon he would. You got a mite dirty when he throwed you out. Reckon you'd be wantin' a bath and to clean up. Looks to me like you ain't got far to go anyway so's you'd best not be tryin' to walk far as the next town."

Geneva nodded. She'd rather eat bugs as admit a thing in front of that miserable excuse for a man who might have even ridden with Sherman when he burned all those lovely homes. She'd watched one of them go up in flames, watched from the tinker's wagon hidden away in a grove of trees as those wicked men set fire to the house. Somehow that day seemed even worse than hiding in the basement and feeling the heat of Hiriam's house burning above her.

"Well, I'd be on the way to the next plantation over to be with my daughter whilst she births my gran'baby. Be gone a month, maybe six weeks. About a mile up that path right there is what's left of the Massa's big old farm. He'd be dead now. Wife too. That bad man burned up the big house but the little houses us slaves had is still standin'. I been livin' in one of them. You'd be right welcome to stay in it. I turned the cow out to pasture and the hogs are rootin' wild. But you could bring them back to the pens if you'd a mind to have some milk or butcher a hog for meat. I might not even come back if the folks what bought up the farm where my daughter's man is workin' will hire an old black woman like me to cook for 'em. Y'all just make y'selves at home and use up whatever you can. Better be used than the tax men come and carry it off in the fall."

"Thank you," Reed said graciously extending his hand to the woman.

"Yes, ma'am," Geneva did the same.

"Right glad to be of help. Long as you ain't from them men who ruined the land and the houses down here," she said.

"No, ma'am. Just a couple of tinkers down on their luck," Geneva said.

"Tinkers. Well, if that don't beat all. Had a tinker by the name of Daniel O'Grady stayin' over at the next plantation last winter. He fixed up a few of my pots 'fore he died. Said come spring he was goin' down Savannah way to see his daughter but the winter fever got him. Well, best be gettin' on my way. Take me till up around dinnertime to walk all the way to my daughter's. Y'all use up whatever you can find. And don't you walk too fast young lady," the woman shook her finger at Geneva.

"Yes, ma'am," Geneva nodded seriously.

"Why'd you lie for me?" Reed asked when the woman was out of hearing distance.

"I need a place to stay. It would have taken a band of angels singing gospel hymns to convince her that I'm not with you, so if you were a Yankee, then I'd be one too and I'd rather be thrown in a cellar of spiders and rattlesnakes as let anyone think that about me," she said as she started off down the pathway, holding her aching back as she went.

"Wait a minute," Reed grabbed the trunk by the leather handle on one end, dragging it along behind him.

"I'm going to find that house and have me a bath, Yank. I ain't waitin' on you. If you can't keep up then leave that trunk behind," she smarted off. Then the full impact of what the old ex-slave woman had said pierced her heart like a dagger slicing through softened butter. Daniel O'Grady had died. Her father was dead. Even if he had given her to Hiriam for gambling debts, he'd been her father.

In less than twenty-four hours she'd watched the Klan hang her husband and now she'd found out her father had passed on. Yet, still there was nothing in her heart but a big ball of anger.

Chapter Three

The one room cabin was scrubbed clean and furnished sparsely. Quilts that had seen better days covered a bed shoved against one wall. Three boards tacked up on the wall beside a window with no glass served as kitchen cabinets: one patched coffee pot, one pan and a heavy skillet, two chipped plates and a couple of cups were arranged neatly. Rough benches flanked the sides of a table with a wash basin and pitcher in the middle of it. A small fireplace on one end furnished heat and a place to cook inside during bad weather. Two calico dresses hung on a nail beside the back door. Geneva was so glad to see them she didn't even think about why the woman hadn't taken them with her. She pulled one down and checked it for size, moaning aloud when she realized it would never fit around her.

"Guess it didn't fit her either or she'd have had it

tied up in one of those pillow cases slung over her shoulder," Reed said from the doorway.

"You can stay in one of the other quarters," she told him, bluntly.

"Well, I sure didn't intend to stay in this mansion with you," he tipped his hat formally and dragged his trunk to the next door. Just who did that woman think she was anyway? Looking at him as if he was dirt on her shoes. He threw open the door to find a small room not so very different from the one where he'd left the woman. What had she said her name was when that woman had awakened them? Geneva. Not that it mattered one bit. Tomorrow morning, with or without Geneva tagging along behind him, he was walking to Ridgeland and catching the next stage-coach north. Using firewood he found stacked neatly beside the fireplace, he stoked up a blaze, found a measure of coffee among the supplies in his trunk and started a pot.

Empty metal field cup in hand, waiting for the coffee to brew, Reed stood in the doorway gazing out across what would have been acres and acres of cotton or tobacco several years ago. Now it lay in disgrace. The big house was nothing more than a pile of blackened rubble with four stone chimneys rising up against the clear blue sky, testimony that people had lived there, cooked there, and warmed their hands by the fire. Laughed. Lived. Gave birth to generations of children. Died. Went to war. Had their way of life ripped apart. At least his home in Love's Valley had survived the violent storm called war. His two brothers had come through the years alive. Three Hamilton men, all alive and well. That alone was a miracle. Not many families had such a blessing. Most of them had sent sons; nearly all of them had lost sons; some of them had no sons coming home.

Carrying his empty cup he began surveying what was left of the plantation gone to ruin. A well house with good cold water. At least Sherman hadn't filled it in with sand and rocks. A smoke house, bare as bleached bones. A sty where the ex-slaves had penned up a few hogs, one old sow still rooting around in the wallow. Reed carefully wired the gate shut. If Geneva decided to stay around she might be interested in having a pig in a pen. A jersey cow peeked around the end of the long line of barracks that had served as slave's quarters for years and years. She bawled at him but didn't attempt to run away when he approached her. A young calf romped out in the green pasture behind the long line of unpainted ramble shack barracks. Evidently he'd had his morning fill of fresh milk but the cow was letting Reed know in no uncertain terms that her udders were still full and aching. Grabbing the rope collar complete with a rusty bell around her neck, he led her to the shed beside the pig sty and found a milk bucket on a far wall. In a few minutes it was full. He carried it and his coffee mug to the well house where he found everything he needed. A clean cheese cloth hanging on a ladder back chair with no bottom. A sparkling clean gallon jar and a cold well of water to lower the milk into to chill it.

By the time he finished the chore and meandered

back to his quarters the sun was high in the sky and his stomach grumbling. The coffee had boiled down to a perfect tarry substance. Hot as the handle on the furnace in the middle of hell. Strong enough to wake up a soldier after only an hour of sleep. Thick enough to hold up a pitchfork. Those were the three qualities the general looked for. Anything else was nothing more than colored water. He poured his cup full and stepped back outside.

The door to the place Geneva had commandeered swung open and she tossed a pan full of dirty water out without looking.

"Good grief, woman, you almost threw that right on me," he shouted.

"Don't raise your voice to me," she shook her finger under his nose. "I'm a human being and the sun was in my eyes. Dinner is almost ready. Come in and wash your hands."

Her voice was soft and Southern even if it had no warmth in it. She still wore the ratty, tattered dress but she'd washed the smut from her face and hands, and Reed was amazed at the difference. Long, freshly washed, blond hair had been braided into two ropes that hung on either side of her massive breasts and stomach all the way to her waist. Eyes, the color of a summer sky, set in a face so beautiful it would have taken any man's breath away. It seemed a shame to put such a gorgeous face on a body like that, but then Reed had always expected that God had a strange sense of humor. How else could one explain the oldest of the Hamilton boys falling in love with a Texan.

Or that the other brother would wind up with a wife from the bayous of Louisiana a few months ago. Yes, sir, God had a sense of humor, all right. Geneva's face belonged on a woman with a slim, graceful body.

"I milked the cow," he said as he washed his hands in the basin she'd refilled with cool water.

"We can have cold milk for supper. I can't abide it warm, though. Got water to drink with your dinner. Couldn't find any coffee or tea or sugar. I guess you must carry some with you but don't worry, I won't be asking you to share it. I hate coffee. Tomorrow morning I'll make gravy to go with the biscuits. Found a half a sack of flour the lady left behind. You can sit there." She pointed to the far side of the table.

He nodded and waited for her to sit before he did.

"It's just a stew. There's a few jars of either beef or venison. I can't tell which it is. Not that it matters. It's all meat. I used one of them and a jar of carrots, found some potatoes about to go to seed in a basket over there. Opened a jar of peaches for dessert. It will fill our stomachs. I suppose you'll be leaving tomorrow after breakfast?" she asked as she filled his bowl.

"Planned on it. Would leave right now but I reckon it'll take all day to walk into Ridgeland. Might as well start out on a full stomach and have the whole day to get there so I don't have to sleep out in the open." He filled his mouth with stew. "This is very good for makeshift soup. Are you going to walk into town with me?" He swallowed and picked up the cup of water, hoping she would tell him she had no intentions of walking all the way to Ridgeland.

"Thank you," she nodded. She could stay hidden away for months on the deserted plantation. Maybe until the first of the year when the tax men came to take whatever was left. By then she'd be able to walk to Ridgeland for sure. "I'm of a mind to stay on right here for a while. I'll fix enough breakfast to send some biscuits along with you tomorrow morning."

"That would be nice," he said, stiffly.

A million questions filtered through his mind, but he didn't ask a single one of them. Curiosity would have to go unsatisfied. He didn't want to know Geneva any better than he did. They were just two strangers who happened to have been thrown together on a stage that got robbed. They'd have a couple of meals together and then go their separate ways. In a few years she'd just be part of a story he'd tell his nieces and nephews about the journey home from his assignment in the middle of rebel territory after the big Civil War.

Geneva ate in silence. Enough had been said.

He was leaving.

She was staying.

Geneva pulled the filthy dress over her head and dropped it into the basin of water, lathered it up with a piece of hard lye soap and set about washing away the dirt and grime. The wash basin had been patched right in the middle of the bottom. Had Daniel been the one who repaired it? Her father—the loquacious, Daniel O'Grady—dead. Hiriam—dead. The first tears rolled down her cheeks as she rubbed harder and harder, trying to wash away the images engraved on her brain: the night her father awoke her with the news Hiriam now owned her but was going to marry her to make it legal, the whole horrid past year of marriage to Hiriam. The dress finally became reasonably clean. The soap couldn't erase what lay so heavy on her heart.

She stripped all the way down to her chemise and lay on the top of the bed, not bothering to turn back the quilts. A gentle, summer breeze flowed through the window, reminding her of the innocence of youth. Of when she and her parents traveled in the wagon. Selling cookware, lace, needles. Repairing pans, tools, wagon wheels. Constantly moving. Except in the winter when they'd meet up with the other traveling people to circle up their wagons beside a creek or a river and wait out the cold. Then the war came and changed all that. No one had money to buy anything or repair what they did have.

She shifted her weight to one side to ease the ache in her back. Destiny decides the inevitable course of life and love. At least that's what her mother had often told her before she died. She always ended her story about how she'd run off with Daniel O'Grady to live the life of the Tuatha'an with that adage. Geneva disagreed. Men decided the course of life and love. Men like Daniel O'Grady, handsome beyond words, a charmer of the highest degree, who couldn't survive without a woman like Geneva's mother to keep his ego inflated; who'd bargain with his own daughter to keep gambling with a rich plantation owner. Men like Hiriam, who'd sell out his own wife to the Klan to save his sorry neck. No, destiny didn't play any part in the course of life and love. Mere men took care of that business.

Reed lay on his back not twenty feet from Geneva. Tension thicker than the two walls that separated them still filled the air. Supper was eaten without a word. She'd spent the evening behind a closed door. He'd spent it sitting on the stoop watching the day melt away into dusk. Now he could hear her sighs and the bed rustling every time she moved. Somehow noise had no problem cutting through tension. He wondered what she was thinking about. Where she'd come from. Where she was running to. The same summer breeze that swept across his bare chest cooled her skin. Did she appreciate even that as much as he did? He laced his fingers behind his head, staring out the window at the stars. Love's Valley, nestled down between two mountains would have the same stars above it. In a few weeks he'd be there, looking at those same stars, but surrounded by his family. The war over. All the Hamilton men back home where they belonged. In a few years the war would be a page in a history book instead of a raw wound in the hearts of the men who had fought for either side.

He dreamed of his best friend, a doctor, who saw even more atrocities of war than Reed had seen. Mitchell, the quiet man from New York City who'd amputated legs and arms, who'd thought it an ironic moment the night he'd delivered a baby boy to one of the women who hung around the army camp. To bring

an innocent life into a world full of chaos and wreck-
age was insanity, he'd told Reed.

In the dream, Mitchell was amputating a soldier's
leg right below the knee. Gangrene had set in and
there was no other option. The young man wept and
Reed held his hand as Mitchell applied the anesthetic,
telling the soldier all the while that he was a lucky
man there was still anesthetic to be had, otherwise the
leg would have had to come off without anything to
deaden the pain.

The man moaned in the dream and Reed awoke, a
fine sheen of sweet covering his face and chest, running down the sides of his forehead and onto the
feather pillow. The man moaned again, a screeching
groan, and Reed sat straight up in bed. The stars were
gone, erased by a sliver of orange on the horizon.
Another grunting moan coupled with weeping. He
shook his head to make sure he was awake and not just
dreaming that he'd awakened from the nightmare.

Crickets serenading, tree toads chiming in, a gut-
tural groan from the cabin next to his. "I'm awake all
right," he mumbled.

"Oh please," he heard Geneva gasp.

She was drowning in a nightmare she couldn't run
from. Before he could decide whether or not to wake
her, she let out another screech that made his skin
crawl. He reached for his shirt and buttoned it as he
opened the door to his cabin and crossed the narrow
distance to her door. He didn't even knock, just slung
it open, expecting to find her thrashing about in her
bed, and trying to awaken from the dream.

He found her propped on two pillows, her legs drawn apart and practically up to her chin as she closed her eyes tightly and huffed like a puppy dog after it had run around the house a dozen times.

"What are you doing?" he asked, not going any closer.

"Get out of here," she demanded.

Rivulets of pure sweat poured from her face, dripping onto the already drenched chemise. Another racking pain took control of her body, demanding her attention. The Yankee shouldn't be there. She could take care of herself. She didn't need him. She didn't need anyone.

"No, I'm not leaving. Are you ill, Geneva? What is the matter with you?" He crossed the room and checked her forehead for fever. Sweaty but cool.

"It's coming," she moaned. "Have you ever delivered a baby, Yankee?"

"A baby?" The room spun out of control. "Are you having a baby? Good Lord, woman, I thought you were just fat."

"Well, thank you for that. And no, I'm not having a baby, I'm having an elephant from the feel of it," she grabbed his hand and squeezed until his knuckles popped.

He remembered that night he'd gone over to the infirmary to see Mitchell. It was the night he'd brought that baby into the world. The other doctors were busy. He'd enlisted Reed's help in the delivery. Mostly what he'd done was stand beside Mitchell and watch. Not so much different from delivering a calf, he'd thought at the time. Except a baby came out head first and calves put their front hooves out first.

"I've got the water ready if the child lives," she said. "Knife is clean and has been boiled to kill germs off it to cut the cord . . ."

She squeezed again and pushed with all her might. "It's coming . . . things laid out over there. Knew it was coming . . ."

He pulled his hand free and rolled up his sleeves.

Twenty minutes later he laid a perfectly formed, very small baby girl in her mother's arms. "Now I'm going to turn you slightly so I can get all this soiled bedding away from you. I'll remake your bed with what's on my bed," he said, his voice calm; his insides a bowl of pure quivering jelly.

"It's a girl?" she asked for the second time as she peered into the swaddling blanket Reed had made by wrapping the baby in one of the dresses hanging on the nail beside the back door.

"Yes, it's a girl," he said.

"Are you a doctor?" Geneva asked sleepily, drawing the baby near her heart.

"No, but I assisted a doctor one time with a delivery so I kind of knew what to do," he said, disappearing out the door, only to return seconds later with an armful of bedding tucked under one arm.

"What are you doing standing up?" he asked, incredulously.

"I'm going to change out of this nasty chemise as soon as you fix that bed," she said as she swayed toward him.

He caught her before she crumpled into a heap on the floor. "Whoa, lady. I think you'd better lie back down."

"Fix the beds," she eased herself onto one of the benches. "Fill that basin, and get out."

"Yes, ma'am," he said, doing what he was told as quickly as he could. Lord Almighty, if they'd let the Southern women fight in the war, it might really have only lasted two months. If they could give birth and stand on their own two feet in less than an hour, then they could have probably fought a battle in the morning, had a leg or arm amputated at noon, and fixed supper for their men folks that evening.

"I'll be back in five minutes to make sure you are back in the bed," he said.

"I can take care of myself. Go on to Ridgeland."

"Sure, I will, and leave you here with a new baby as weak as a motherless lamb," he snapped. "Get yourself cleaned up however you want to and I'll be back in five minutes unless I hear a thump where you've fallen on the floor. I'm not real anxious to raise up a baby without a mother," he took the child from her arms and laid it on the clean bed.

Five minutes lasted just short of eternity as he checked his pocket watch every ten seconds. He heard her moving around very slowly. Heard the baby whimper. Heard her tell the little girl child to be patient, then heard the heavy sigh as she lowered herself back into the bed. Using one of the calico dresses hanging on a nail as a blanket, she offered the newborn her first meal. The baby latched on and sucked hungrily. She might be early but she full well was ready to step up to the plate and take her breakfast.

"That's the spirit, child. Don't ever let anyone take that from you," Geneva peeped under the faded calico to find a head full of downy blond fuzz and the delicate features she remembered from her own mother's younger days.

"Now where is that sack of flour you found?" Reed plowed inside, his presence filling the room with an electrical force. "I'm hungry and you've put in quite a night's work so I'll make breakfast."

"Then you'll leave?" she asked.

"Then I'll stay a few more days until you get on your feet real good. When Mother had Indigo, Daddy said she had to stay abed six weeks. She laughed at him and said no more than six days. I expect in a week you'll be ready to take over your own cooking and washing. Until then I'll stick around," he said as he pulled down the biggest pan and poured the flour into it. "I'll make a big batch."

He was surprisingly adept for a man in the kitchen. Stoked up a fire, put the biscuits in the iron skillet and hurried outside for the milk to make gravy. Geneva figured he'd get sidetracked and they'd have burned biscuits, but she was wrong. He made perfect gravy, pinched her biscuits into bite-sized pieces, covered them with creamy gravy and sat down at the edge of the bed to feed her.

"Good lord, I can feed myself," she said. "I've had a baby, not lost the use of my arms. Just prop the pillows behind me, if you would, please."

"Baby finished and sleeping yet?" Reed asked.

"Yes, she is," Geneva laid the child gently to one side, careful to keep her wrapped but to also keep her nose free so she could breathe.

"So where's the baby's daddy?" Reed asked, handing Geneva the plate.

"Dead," Geneva filled her mouth with biscuits and gravy, thinking it was the best food she'd ever eaten.

"War?" Reed asked, as he filled his own plate and sat down to the table.

"Klan," she said bluntly. "The morning I boarded the stagecoach. They were looking for me but hung him instead."

"Just yesterday?" His hand stopped midair and he stared at her.

"I don't want to talk about it," she said. "It's over."

Shock. The woman was in pure, unadulterated, genuine shock. Her husband dead. Running from the Klan. What on earth had Harry Reed Hamilton gotten himself tangled up with.

"I think we'd better talk about it," he said. "We need to get you back to Savannah to your family. We need to tell the authorities."

"My family is all dead. I'm one of the Tuatha'an— the traveling people. Tinkers, you might know us as. I've an aunt in Lynchburg, Virginia. I'll go there when I'm able. The Klan was the sheriff, a couple of deputies, and the mayor. Might as well not tell them anything. And that's all I've got to say. Like I said before, it's over."

Reed nodded briefly. He'd stay a week. No self-respecting gentleman, Yankee or Rebel, would leave a woman and a brand-new baby out here in the middle of nowhere with no family or friends. He didn't need to know any more of her story. Didn't need to know why she didn't grieve for the father of her child.

"What you going to name her?" he asked, changing the subject.

"I don't know yet. I didn't even want her yesterday. Hoped she'd be born dead with the blood she had in her veins. But somewhere through the night I changed my mind. I'd fight a war for her and no one is ever going to gamble with her life. I promised her that right before she was born. If it was a boy, he was going to respect women. If it was a girl, she was going to grow up loved. What's your mother's name?" Geneva asked.

"Laura," Reed said, a tickle of apprehension raising the hair on his neck.

"Mine was Eva. That's why my father named me Geneva—a longer form of Eva. Her name is Eva Laura, then. I'll give her your mother's name since you helped me bring her into the world. You can tell your mother that when you get back to your home, Yank."

For some reason, Reed didn't think he'd ever tell his mother any such thing. His brothers both had wives who'd want to use family names for their children. Reed didn't think his mother would be impressed that a woman who didn't even want her child would name her Laura.

"I could sleep now," Geneva said. "Eva and I could take a long nap. I suppose you'll milk the cow?"

"Yes, and take care of things so you'll be comfortable when I leave," he said.

"Good. One week and you'll be gone," she snuggled the baby next to her and shut her eyes.

Chapter Four

Lying abed in the middle of the day seemed sinful to Geneva. Not one time in her whole life had she ever seen her mother in bed after sunrise. Not until that last week, at least, when the fever took her. She unwrapped the baby girl and counted her fingers and toes, amazed that something as loathsome as the past year could have produced a perfectly formed baby. *Destiny decides the inevitable course of life and love,* she thought as she looked into the unblinking, wide open eyes of her daughter.

"Ready for supper?" Reed didn't even rap on the unpainted, weathered door frame.

"I'm starving," Geneva said. "And I've decided to rename this baby. She isn't Eva Laura after all. She's only going to have one name and that's Destiny."

"Kind of strange for a baby. Destiny is just a shortened form of destination. Another word for it is

41

future," he peered down at the scrawny bit of flesh snuggled up tightly in Geneva's arms.

"My mother said that destiny decides the inevitable course of life and love. Her name is Destiny. No middle name. Just one name. She can decide her own course of life and love, which is more than most women get to do. I'm going to teach her that every day of her life. No man is ever going to own Destiny," Geneva said.

"Want to talk about it?" Reed asked.

"No, it's over, like I said. And yes, I'm hungry," she didn't smile.

But then Reed scarcely expected her to smile. Great wonder her mind wasn't affected. Seeing the Klan hang her husband, running away like that, and then giving birth, all in the space of less than twenty-four hours.

He heated the stew he'd made earlier in the day. A replica of the one she'd made the day before. There were still four biscuits left from the previous two meals, so he laid two on the edge of her plate and carried it to her bedside.

"Thank you," she murmured. Even that was hard to spit out to a Yankee.

"You are welcome, Geneva," he said, sitting down at the table to eat his food. Time was in the field when the men would have fought rattlesnakes and raging rebels for a plate of stew like that. When they'd fantasized about a beef roast with potatoes and carrots cooked along side it. But fantasies didn't produce hot meals. Mostly what they did was scrape mold from bread and swallow it hurriedly, washing it down with a cup of the general's thick coffee. Time was, also, when they went days without either, wishing for something other than cold creek water to fill their aching bellies.

He'd swallowed his last bite and was down to the dregs of lukewarm coffee when he heard the wagon approaching. His heart fairly well leaped up to his chest. Someone had apprehended the stage robbers and then come to rescue him and Geneva. The ordeal was over.

"Hey, y'all in there," he heard someone yell and almost upset the table getting to the door.

"We're here," he yelled out into the dusk. "Right here."

"That'd be good," the black woman eased her bulky frame from the wagon seat. "I'd be comin' back to get my stuff. Big man over there made me the cook. Daughter's man here got use of the wagon to bring my stuff. Got a cabin bigger'n this one. Two whole rooms for just me. Got to hurry up. Got to cook the mornin' meal for them. They's just bought the place. Year ago they'd be poor white trash, now they big plantation owners."

Reed's heart fell to his knees.

"Wife of yours have that baby?" The woman crossed the dirt yard to the door. "I'll swanee, but she did. I knowed when I seen her she'd be havin' it soon. I'm gatherin' my things to take to the new cabin," she told Geneva as she picked up the cookware from the shelves.

"Do you need the bed?" Geneva asked.

"No, you just stay right there. I'll take one from one of the other places. Keep those quilts too. I'll get the ones on the line. What you got there wrapped up in one of my daughter's old dresses?"

"It's a girl. Her name is Destiny," Geneva unwrapped the baby for the woman to see.

"Fine little thing. All there even if she'd be a mite little. Like that name. Don't sound like somethin' no white woman would be namin' her baby though." The woman turned to the huge black man blocking the door. "Isaac, you go tie the cow and the sow to the back of the wagon and fetch up a bed from one of the other places. My daughter has got lots of food over there so I'll be leavin' the cannin', what there's left of it. That'll keep you till you're able to be goin' on ahead. There's a trunk down in the last cabin that's got some baby things in it. 'Fore the big house burned down to the ground, the missus, she stored a bunch of stuff in that cabin. Mostly just her old things and the baby things from when her boys was little. We done used up most of her clothes. Isaac, you come on in here and get my pans." She scraped away at the two plates Geneva and Reed had just used, rinsed them hurriedly in the wash basin and dried them on her apron tail.

"I'd be willing to pay you handsomely for that team of mules and the wagon out there to take Geneva and the baby on to Ridgeland. Or better yet, I'll give you the price of the rig to take us there," Reed said.

"No, sir," Isaac shook his head. "Me and my wife,

we been lookin' for work a long time. This here rig, it belongs to the new owners what hired us. We got loan of it but we got to get it right back. I wouldn't be doin' nothin' that would lose me that job."

"I see," Reed said.

"Besides, this woman ain't ready to be ridin' in no wagon," the woman declared with a shake of all her chins. "This place might be sellin' to new owners right soon. Folks is startin' to buy the land for taxes. Those what made some money on the war, that is. The old Southern folks, why, their luck done run out. Never know. New boss man might have a job for you and you won't need to be goin' nowhere after all."

"Thank you for leaving the bed," Geneva said.

"You'd be welcome," the woman crawled back up on the wagon and Isaac snapped the reins. They rode off into the dusk, the cow bawling, the sow snorting, and the calf romping along behind as if it were all a big picnic.

Reed watched them until there wasn't even a puff of dust on the horizon. Not so very long ago he would have commandeered the wagon and mules, but the war was over.

"Well?" Geneva said from behind him.

"Well, what?" he snapped.

"There's a trunk full of baby things hiding down the slave quarters. It would be nice to have them. Should you hold Destiny while I go get them or should I just keep her here in my arms and you go find them?" she snipped right back at him. Yankees! How in the world did they ever win the war, anyway? Their heads were thick as hundred-year-old oak trees, and their brains would fit into one of her mother's thimbles, all of which were lost in the fire. . . . She fought back a whole swarm of tears as she suddenly remembered the few keepsakes she'd lost when she walked away from Savannah.

"There is no need to cry. I'll find your trunk," he said.

"I'm not crying," she said between clenched teeth. "And if I was, it sure wouldn't be to impress you."

"Good, because let it be known right now that I am willing to stay here and help you for a week, but after that I'm leaving," he said, turning his back and stepping out into the hot night air. Good grief, how was he supposed to find anything in the cabins in the dark. *You are a soldier and a spy. You found Rebel camps in the dark.* His conscience reminded him bluntly.

"Clumsy as they were, it was a picnic. Finding a trunk full of baby things. That's a different matter," he mumbled as he went to his own room, groaned when he saw the bare straw-filled mattress and rooted around blindly in his own trunk for a candle.

He found a pan in the first cabin and set in on the stoop. A musty smelling quilt in another. Tomorrow he'd wash it and at least have something to put between him and the mattress ticking. A chipped bowl in another. A cracked plate in still another. When he shoved open the last door he found the treasure. Three old trunks. One, just as the woman said, filled to the brim with baby clothes. Most yellow with age, but still hanging together. Another trunk was filled with diaries.

Years and years worth of neat handwriting. Promising himself he'd return tomorrow to read what had gone on at the big house before fire had taken away its dignity, he opened the final trunk to find it half full of outdated ladies' dresses. Things he remembered seeing his mother wear when he was a little boy, when he had romped up and down Love's Valley with his brothers. Nostalgia filled his broad chest as he hugged one of the frocks to his face, not even minding the musty smell of it. Shaking the past out of his head with a fierce jolt, he gently laid the dress back in the trunk and shut the lid. He'd be home soon and he'd hug his mother for real.

Hoisting the baby trunk on his shoulder he blew out the candle and made his way back down to the cabin where the dim light flowed through the open window. A mosquito the size of a small buzzard landed on his cheek. Using his free shoulder to rub it away, he wondered about Destiny. He should hang something over that window so the bugs wouldn't eat up her skin.

"What took you so long?" Geneva asked when he set the trunk on the table and threw it open.

"I had to battle a mosquito," he said. "Things are all old and smell like they've been stored forever."

"The mosquitoes or the baby clothes?" Geneva asked, easing her long legs over the side of the bed and cautiously standing up. The room did a couple of funny spins but then settled down. She held onto the wall and made her way to the table where she quickly sunk onto one of the benches.

"Need some help?" Reed asked from the other side of the trunk.

"No, Mr. Hamilton, I can take care of myself. You could leave right now and I would manage fine," she said.

"Okay," he said, "then I'm going over to my luxurious hotel room to bed."

"Set the trunk on the floor before you leave, please," she said.

"Oh, the great iron maiden can't throw the trunk off the table? I thought you could fight a forest fire all by yourself," he taunted.

"Get out. I'll do it without your help," she said.

Her eyes reminded him of January in Love's Valley. Bitter cold. Snow, hip deep. Wind whistling through the bare trees. Not enough coats and hats in the world to keep a man warm from her glare. If he didn't set the trunk down, she would, even if it killed her. Then he'd feel bound by honor to try to take care of that sleeping bundle on the bed, with no cow for milk. Somehow he didn't think little Destiny—what a horrid name to put upon a child; sounded like a slave's name—would be able to digest venison stew.

He grabbed the trunk, sat it at her feet, opened it with silent ceremony and a flourish of fury, and then promptly left the room. Berating himself for letting a piece of Southern fluff get under his skin, he threw himself on the bare bed and laced his hands behind his head. One of those monstrous mosquitoes born in the South Carolina swampland lit on his arm, thinking to drain him of half his life's blood. He slapped at it, leaving a silver dollar sized blob of red. What if one of those merciless critters landed on Destiny? He'd meant to cover the window and had forgotten in the argument. That woman had the warmth of an iceberg and a tongue sharper than a freshly honed butcher knife. To go back in there would be admitting defeat. But to let the baby suffer wasn't fair.

He heard water sloshing. Surely that crazy woman wasn't doing laundry at this time of night. He was off the bed and standing in her open doorway before he realized what he was doing.

Geneva looked up from the wash basin. She was a tall woman. Almost six feet tall. That's what had turned many of the tinkers away from her when she was sixteen and considered ready to wed. No one wanted a woman a full head taller than he was. Men wanted a tiny, little slip of nothing so they could feel big and glorious in their masculinity. At eighteen, no one had stepped up to claim her hand. At twenty, her father began to complain about the disgrace of having an old maid for a daughter. It didn't make her one inch shorter. At twenty-two, she'd been lost to Hiriam in a game of poker. But even with her height, she sure didn't look down on Harry Reed Hamilton. He was half a head taller than she, and had a chest as broad as half an acre of cotton land, and covered with the softest looking furry, curly hair she'd ever seen.

"What are you doing?" he asked.

"I'm going to wash out a few of these things to put on Destiny come morning. Hot as it is, they'll be dry by then and won't smell so bad," she said, feeling high color filling her cheeks and a prickly sensation on her neck. Must be what happened to women after they'd given birth, she figured. Even though he'd helped with the delivery, she was embarrassed to tell him there were other things from the trunk that she needed as a new mother. Things to take care of herself after a birthing. And they needed washing as much or more than the nappies and tiny little baby shirts.

"You only had that child this morning, Geneva. Go on back to your bed. I'll wash the things for you," he said but his voice carried no warmth.

"I'll help. I can do it sitting on the bench and I'm tired of layin'," she said. "I can wash them and lay them aside. Then if you would throw out the water and get rinse water from the well, I can rinse the soap out of them. If you'd hang them on the line outside, the night air is hot enough to dry them by morning," she said.

"You should have gone into the war. You'd have made a good general," he sat down across the table from where she'd begun to rub lye soap into the water.

"Size was right. Gender wasn't," she said.

He bit his tongue to keep the retort back and watched her deftly clean hemmed flannel nappies, along with the tiniest of gowns and a bonnet or two. Several blankets came next and then more flannel, not quite as big as the first nappies. Must be for belly binders, he surmised, remembering the way his mother had pinned such things around Indigo when she was born. He wondered if boy babies had belly binders wrapped around their stomachs until the cord fell off. Or was it just newborn girls that needed them.

He didn't remember Mitch telling that new mother to use them when he delivered her son.

Geneva and Reed both kept silent as she worked. When she had a pile the size of a bushel basket on the end of the table, he threw the basin of water out the door and refilled it with clean, cool water from the well. Three times he threw water out the door before Geneva was satisfied everything was soap free. The things sure weren't as nice as what she had gotten ready for the new baby in Hiriam's house. He'd spared no expense for the new son, demanding that everything she sewed for the upcoming child be made for a boy, embroidered in blue. No pink. No flowers of any kind on the blankets. Hiriam's son was going to be a man's man. He'd raise him to hunt and fish and take care of his plantation. A smile tickled the corners of Geneva's mouth. Hiriam didn't hunt and fish. He played cards and sipped whiskey all day and into the night if anyone would play or drink with him. A son would have had as much chance of reversing the effects of the war as making Hiriam go hunting and fishing. Hiriam would have been devastated to know the only child he'd produced was nothing more than a girl.

The moon was high in the sky when Reed laced his hands behind his head for the second time that night. She must have been really happy with all that the trunk produced because one time she'd almost smiled. Almost, not quite. And it didn't reach her eyes.

Geneva gingerly eased herself back on the bed at

the same time Destiny whimpered for another feeding. Geneva bared her breast and an enormous mosquito landed on it, hungry for his own supper. She swatted it and covered the baby well so the bugs wouldn't get to her. Tomorrow she'd ask Reed to figure out something to do with the window and doorway. It might cut down on the airflow but she couldn't have her child eaten alive by swamp mosquitoes. Deep lines furrowed across her forehead as she frowned. She wouldn't ask that man to do one thing. By tomorrow she'd be stronger and she'd figure out something to do on her own. Maybe there was mosquito netting down in the bottom of the trunk. The rich people always had it to drape around their babies' cradles. Hopefully there would be enough to cover the window and the door.

Destiny ate hungrily for several minutes then Geneva popped the breast from her mouth and laid her up on her shoulder, patting her back gently. To think that she'd prayed that the baby would be born dead the night she rode in the stagecoach. That she'd seen it as some kind of devil spawned by Hiriam. Not so. Instead, Destiny was an angel sent the day after a catastrophe to bring peace to Geneva. How it had happened, she couldn't begin to explain, but sitting there in old slave quarters on a homemade bed, with nothing but hand-me-down clothing and a ragged quilt to cover with, she was at peace.

"Go to sleep little angel," she crooned. "Maybe I should rename you again. Maybe you should be Angelina. Who'd have ever thought I could even pick your name. Hiriam had your name all ready. Hiriam Mason Garner IV. I wonder what he would have named a girl. But you are my first bit of freedom. I can do what I want. Destiny sounds good since I do want you to be in control of your life. But Angelina sounds even better. I think you are an Angelina, little baby girl. An angel would surely have control of their life as well as every life they touch. I'll tell the Yankee in the morning," she whispered, easing back down into the pillows and falling fast asleep.

This time she didn't dream of white sheets flapping in the wind or of Hiriam's bulging eyes as he hung from the tree. She dreamed of a cool mountain stream and a little blond haired girl's giggles as she threw rocks into the cold, icy water. Even in the dream, as peaceful and beautiful as it was, Geneva stood on the sidelines and knew she was dreaming, but she clamped her eyelids tight, not wanting to wake up and spoil the quiet serenity or stay the bubbling giggles of her daughter, either.

Chapter Five

Geneva laid Angelina in the middle of the narrow bed, easing her down gently so she wouldn't awaken the child. She waited barely a minute to make sure the baby stayed asleep, and then scooted out the backdoor in a hurry to the outhouse. Someday she was going to be so rich she'd have one of those indoor bathrooms. She'd never seen one but of all the things in the world she coveted it was a toilet with light and no spiders.

Reed picked up his rifle and set out across the yard, hoping to catch sight of a rabbit or two. He'd killed two yesterday and spit-cooked them over an open fire in the yard. Geneva had even said they were a welcome change from stew made from canned meat. They'd come to an unspoken arrangement after the first couple of days when she insisted she was tired of lying abed. She cooked most of the meals. He helped with cleanup and laundry. They hadn't made any fast friendship, which was good since tomorrow he was going to Ridgeland and she was staying at the plantation alone. He scanned the edge of the woods at the far edge of the property, thinking he might even see a deer. In a day's time he could dress out a small one, leaving her well-fixed with fresh meat for a week or more. Maybe he'd even fire up the smoke house and hang the hind quarters up to cure.

He didn't see anything, not even a stirring in the trees to give him hope there was a deer rattling around somewhere close. He turned and looked back toward the house in time to see Geneva make a trot down the back pathway toward the outhouse, Straining his ears, he didn't hear the baby whimpering so she must be sleeping.

Angelina. After three tries, the name finally seemed final. To tell the truth he was glad Geneva had changed it from Eva Laura. Somehow, naming a child he had no intentions of laying eyes on again after his mother wasn't right. Then that next name, Destiny, because of something her mother used to say, was simply horrible. No one named a child something like that. At least Angelina was a real name. Not that it mattered a whole lot. From the time Reed had laid her in her mother's arms right after her birth, he'd never touched her again. Geneva kept her wrapped up in some kind of contraption she called a sling. She said slaves used it when they went to the fields. Nothing more than a piece of cloth, she wrapped it over one shoulder and knotted it on the opposite hip. She tucked the baby there inside it, going about her work and feeding the child at the same time.

She wasn't wearing the sling when he saw her dash off to the outhouse, so evidently she'd left Angelina on the bed asleep. Not that Reed blamed her one bit for doing it either. He could barely imagine being literally saddled with a child all day long but taking a little thing like that into the outhouse—now that wasn't a pretty idea.

A movement coming around the far end of the row of flat-roofed shanties caught his eye. Surely a deer wouldn't wander that close to civilization. He slowly turned his head, adjusting his vision through squinted eyes, without making too much noise or movement. Deer were spooky at best and the slightest whisper of change would send it leaping back toward the woods. Reed raised his rifle and held his breath. What he saw wasn't a deer but an enormous wild hog, trotting along, snorting, sniffing the air, and heading straight for the cabin at the end of the row. The place where it could smell the leftovers from breakfast. The place where a newborn, week-old baby girl was lying unprotected on the bed.

Reed took off in a dead run, screaming at the top of his lungs, hoping to draw the boar's attention to himself and away from the open door where it was already poking its head inside. He should have shot it the first moment he saw it, he berated himself as he ran. But if he'd missed and only wounded it, the boar would have gone wild. There wouldn't have been a chance it wouldn't tear Angelina to shreds if it was wounded.

When Reed stepped inside the door, his gun raised

to his shoulder, the boar was already reared up on the bed, sniffing the edge of Angelina's blanket. As if she sensed that she was no longer wrapped up in her sling right next to her mother's calm, beating heart, she let out a wail and the hog snorted, opening his mouth wide and lowering his big tusks. Reed pulled the trigger, the boom and blood filling the room as the boar squealed one more time and then dropped on the floor.

Reed threw the gun, not even caring where it landed, and gathered the screaming baby into his arms, holding her tightly against his broad chest. "It's all right, baby girl. I killed the big old mean hog. He won't ever scare you again. I promise. I'll take care of you, now don't cry no more," he crooned as he went outside with her.

Geneva heard Reed's screams and wondered for a moment what on earth he was hollering about. She'd never heard him raise his voice, not even when he was angry. He might turn white with rage, set his jaw so firmly that it looked as if he'd break his teeth, draw his eyebrows down into deep furrows and shoot daggers at her, but he'd never come close to raising his voice. Even when she went on one of her tirades about how all men were just alike. Then suddenly there was a boom and Geneva jumped three inches off the wooden seat. She was running toward the house without even knowing how she'd put herself aright. Something was terribly wrong. She could feel it. The gunshot was entirely too near. Rabbits didn't come that close to the front door.

By the time she rounded the end of the cabin, Reed

was coming out the door, holding Angelina with blood covering her blankets. The baby's screams left no doubt she was dying. Reed had killed her child. Geneva had trusted the man. How could he do this?

"It was a wild hog," Reed said above Angelina's howling. "It must have smelled the breakfast odors. It was about to eat the baby. I shot it."

Geneva stared at him blankly and peeked inside the door, to make sure he wasn't lying to her. There was his gun thrown against the fireplace and an enormous hog sprawled out on the floor, shot clean through the head. Blood dripped from Reed onto the floor but the streak on the bed and down the edge left no doubt he was telling the truth. Instead of killing her child, he'd saved her life.

She reached out her arms to take Angelina from him, to make sure the hog hadn't hurt her in any way. A whooshing noise filled her ears, the ground came up to meet her face and she crumpled into a pile of loose connected bones at his feet.

Reed stood there holding a wailing infant who'd just christened his shirt and pants with a wet nappy, and looked at the six-foot woman who had just fainted, literally landing on the toes of his boots. Reluctant to lay the baby down anywhere, and especially not eager to take her back into Geneva's cabin, he finally took her into his own place and laid her on the bed. She gulped in another lungful of air and set up a fresh caterwauling while Reed went back outside to pick Geneva up out of the dirt. Surprised that someone as tall as she

was could weigh so little, he carried her into the room
and lay her on the bed beside the still screeching baby.

When Angelina's demanding temper didn't rouse
her, Reed picked the child up again and rocked her
gently, trying to simulate the way she would feel if she
were wrapped up in the sling. In a few minutes it
worked and Angelina stared at him with big, round
eyes, as if saying she didn't believe he was her mother for an instant. Something in those eyes wrapped
binding cords around Reed's heart, causing it to skip
a beat. So this was the way a new father must feel, he
thought. Then he remembered the real mother
stretched out on his bed. Did women die from a case
of vapors? He didn't have any smelling salts in his
trunk and he didn't know what to do with her. Would
washing her face with a cool cloth help or hinder her
condition? Lord have mercy, his mother had never
fainted a day in her life and his sister, Indigo, was
made of steel and vinegar. She sure would never faint.

As suddenly as they'd shut, Geneva's eyes flew
open and she was on her feet, her arms thrown around
Reed, hugging him tightly, the baby between them,
cooing now and snuggling down even deeper into
Reed's embrace.

"I'm so sorry," Geneva said.

"You couldn't have known," Reed said, uncomfort-
able with the scenario, with the feelings grabbing hold
of his heart like a strong vise grip. "Don't worry,
Geneva. I'll stay on until you are ready to travel. I can't
leave you and Angelina alone. I'll stay and protect you."

No sooner were the words out than he wished he could have taken them back or bitten off his tongue. Heat crept up his neck to flush his face and the urge to shove Angelina into Geneva's arms and run like a scared jackrabbit was so strong he had to fight the impulse away with every scrap of willpower he possessed.

Geneva heard the words but scarcely believed he'd keep his word. That he was ready to be on his way had been evident for days now and tomorrow was the day. From now on she'd just have to keep the doors shut, no matter how stifling hot it got. She'd have to take Angelina with her everywhere including the outhouse. When what he had just said sunk in fully, she realized she was hugging the man. All three of them: Angelina, Reed and Geneva wrapped up like a family who'd just survived a tornado.

Well, we did survive a wild hog, she argued with herself, staying another minute in the safe embrace of his strong arms, liking the way it felt to be protected and safe.

"Hello, the house," a big booming voice yelled from outside.

Reed and Geneva broke away from each other as if they'd been doing something totally immoral and unacceptable. Both of them feeling awkward in the aftermath of the promises Reed had just made and the emotions swirling around in the room like a wind storm.

"Anybody at home?" the voice yelled again.

Reed peeked out the door to find a tinker's brightly

painted wagon sitting not ten feet from him. "We're home," he said hoarsely.

"Mornin'. I'm Liam O'Neal. Told Daniel O'Grady I'd come check on him this summer but the old slave woman over on the next plantation said he'd up and died. But said there was a couple here might be interested in going on to Ridgeland. I'm headin' that way if you'd be a mind to ride along," he said.

"Liam?" Geneva pushed Reed aside, only slightly amazed that the touch of his bare upper arms on her palms was like lightning shooting through her arms. Strange, he'd not affected her like that before. Not even when he'd delivered her child.

"Geneva O'Grady?" Liam grinned. "Is that really you? I heard you'd gone down to Savannah and married up with a rich plantation owner. One of them who didn't get burned out."

"I did but he died," she said, suddenly sheepish around the old man she'd known her whole life. Whose son she'd fancied herself in love with when she was twelve years old. Whose wife had been her mother's best friend. Whose daughter, Sylvie, had been her best friend.

"I'm right sorry," he nodded seriously. "Well, old black woman said you and your husband had yourselves a new baby and something about a stagecoach bein' robbed and you two thrown off it. So you wantin' a ride on to Ridgeland or not?"

"Yes," Reed said. "We would be obliged to you for a ride into Ridgeland. I'd be glad to pay you whatever you want."

"No money necessary. Geneva is liken unto family to me. If I'd a knowed it was her stranded out here, I'd a been here sooner rather than diddling away at this place and that. Take long to get your things together? I reckon we could be there by nightfall if you hurry," Liam asked.

"Five minutes," Geneva said. "I have to get my trunk . . ." she let the sentence trail off, dreading going back into that room where the hog was sprawled out on her floor.

"I'll do it," Reed said. "A wild boar just scared about six years off our lives. It was ready to kill the baby when I got to the door and shot it. I don't think Geneva wants to go back in there. We'll have two trunks. Is there room to take them both?" he asked, already categorizing all the things he could leave behind if the man said no.

"Well . . ." Liam rubbed his chin. "There's a cot back there for Geneva and the baby to ride on and you can come up front with me. There's a bit of room for one trunk. I don't think we could take on two, though. Think you could pack them all into one?"

"I sure can," Reed said. "Give me five minutes and we'll be ready. Geneva, take the baby on in there," he nodded toward his own quarters, "and I'll bring over her things. We'll consolidate it all into one."

"Liam, I am so glad to see you," she touched his arm. "And thank you."

"You're welcome child. Right welcome. Now do like your husband says and take care of gettin' things done," he said.

"Why didn't you tell him that you are not my husband?" she hissed as she picked out what things she'd need for the trip. When they got to Ridgeland, she'd purchase a few more items at the general store to take her on toward Lynchburg.

"Why didn't you?" Reed tossed aside anything he didn't need. "Put Angelina's things in here. When we get to Ridgeland, I'll take you to the store and buy you a couple of decent dresses."

"I have my own money," she said. "You don't owe me anything."

"No, I don't, but I did give you my word and I'll see to it you get to Lynchburg to your aunt's place. It's on my way home anyway. And I don't ever want another man to look at me like I'm dirt because my wife isn't dressed decently," he said, changing his wet shirt for his oldest, most worn one. If Geneva looked like a poor cracker, then he would also.

"I'm not your wife," she snapped.

"I know that. You know that. But it appears no one else does. So unless you want Liam O'Neal to think you've been living with a man you're not married to, then march your sweet little Southern self out there and tell him," Reed tossed aside the wet nappy and blankets she'd taken off Angelina.

Geneva's face flushed scarlet. To let Liam think she was married to Reed was far easier than telling him otherwise and having the story bandied about the Tuatha'an campsite that winter. She could hear it now. The big, tall horse of a woman was sold off as chattel to a man who wound up on the business end of a Klan rope. Then she ran away to save her own skin, gave birth to the man's child, and lived with another man. Yes, the women had been right to keep their sons away from Daniel O'Grady's daughter. But then that's what happened when a Tuatha'an married outside his or her own. And Daniel had done just that. Married a rich, Southern woman, snuck her right out from under her father's nose and tried to make her one of the Tuatha'an. Geneva was proof that mixed marriages did not work.

Geneva shuddered at being the butt of such a story. No, it was simpler to let Liam keep believing what he already did.

"Ready?" Liam asked when Reed hauled his steamer trunk out the door.

"Ready," Reed said, helping Geneva into the back of the wagon. Never before had he looked inside a tinker's wagon and he was amazed at everything inside the confines of the small place. Liam had been right when he said he couldn't take on two trunks. The one barely left room for Geneva's feet when she sat down on the narrow cot.

"Liam," Geneva drew back the curtains covering the window behind where he sat. "Please tell me all about the traveling people. What about Rudy and Sylvie? Where did you winter?" She knew if Liam's started talking he'd go on and on for hours. She'd only have to remember something occasionally to keep him going. If he talked, he wouldn't ask questions.

And that's what she wanted. No questions for her to answer or to have to lie about. She didn't want to talk about Hiriam or even her father. She just wanted a ride into town where she full well intended to relieve one Reed Hamilton of his word to escort her all the way to her aunt's house in Lynchburg, Virginia. Once in civilization where wild boars did not roam about, she'd be fine traveling alone with her child.

Chapter Six

The sound of Reed's boots on the hardwood floor of the hotel sounded like gunshots in the quietness of the evening. The desk clerk, who'd been visiting with the only other person in the room, looked up with a question in his eyes.

"Help you?" he asked.

"Yes, I need—" Reed started to say.

"Excuse me but I was here first, and I'm not finished," the other man turned to scowl at Reed, the silver star on his chest reflecting the candlelight.

"Go right ahead. You were indeed here first," Reed recognized the sheriff from Savannah, Georgia, immediately.

The man barely tilted his head in acknowledgment. "Like I said, I'm looking for a tall, big woman. Name of Geneva Garner. I had to be up here on some other business. Got to pick up a bank robber. But I figure

66

she'll be headed through here so thought I'd check around while I'm waiting. Can't imagine why she hasn't already been seen. Stage was stolen and robbed more than a week ago. Didn't find any bodies so I figure the robbers tossed the passengers out in the swamp."

"You can look right here on the books. Haven't had a woman by that name. Matter of fact, Sheriff, I ain't seen a woman like you described at all. You say she's in the family way. Ain't no decent woman would be traveling like that all the way from Savannah," the desk clerk said.

"She ain't decent. She's one of them tinkers. Old Hiriam wasn't a big man. She must have doped him up or poisoned him before she killed him. I figure she got him in the saddle on the back of a horse and hung him that way. Then she burned down his house. She's wanted for murder and arson. You see her, you just tell the local sheriff and he'll jail her and then telegraph me. I can be up here in a day and pick her up. She'll find out what it's like to hang by the neck until dead. Hiriam was a buddy of mine," the sheriff said. "I'm going down the street to the saloon to have a drink. I'll be back at night though. Leaving out with my prisoner at first light."

A prickly sensation tickled the nape of Reed's neck. Geneva was sleeping soundly in Liam's wagon right outside the hotel. "How much for a room?" Reed asked.

"Two bucks a night. That'd include breakfast since you done missed supper," the desk clerk said.

"No thank you," Reed shook his head. "Haven't got two bucks. Thought maybe it would be cheaper."

"Sorry. You want anything cheaper, you might check with the livery. Sometimes they let drifters stay in the loft for two bits," the man said.

"I'll do that," Reed said, hurrying out the door to find the sheriff already standing beside the wagon.

Reed shouted at Liam. "We won't be staying here. The price is too high. Guess we'll be going on down the road."

"That's the second time you've butted into my conversation tonight," the sheriff turned on him. "You better start learning a little respect. But then that's what you'd expect from a tinker, ain't it?"

"Help you, Sheriff? Have to 'scuse my boy here. He's big but he ain't too bright," Liam's blue eyes, bedded down in a face full of wrinkles fairly well twinkled.

"I just saw you here and thought maybe you might have some information for me. I'm looking for a woman. Tall, big woman. In the family way. She got on a stagecoach in Savannah headed up this way. Stagecoach got robbed and she and the man she was traveling with were tossed out on the road. We've combed the old plantations and haven't been able to find her. Name of Geneva Garner. Come from the tinkers a year ago. You ever heard of her?" the sheriff asked.

Reed stood behind the officer, wishing he could relay the whole story to Liam without giving away anything. But Liam just smiled at him and patted the wagon seat, still warm from Reed riding on it all day. "Get on back up here, son. We'll just go on a ways farther and camp out tonight. I told you that the hotel was way too high for us to be stayin' in when you asked. Now, Sheriff, I wouldn't know anyone by that name. Geneva Garner, you say? Nope, can't say as I've ever heard of no Geneva Garner," Liam rubbed his chin. "What'd you want to find her for anyway?"

"She murdered her husband and set fire to his plantation home. Burned it to the ground," the sheriff said.

"Now ain't that a terrible thing," Liam said. "Sounds somewhat to me like something them men calls themselves the Klan would do," Liam said.

Reed could have strangled the tinker barehanded, watching his eyeballs pop out and roll down the wood sidewalk like a boy's marbles. If he'd shut up then they could be on their way.

"This woman is in the family way and big as a horse. Looker but not one most men would want to marry," the sheriff said.

"Right sorry I can't help you none, sheriff," Liam still didn't make a move to snap the whip and get his horses moving.

Reed began to sweat bullets. He could hear Geneva shushing the baby in the wagon. One shrill cry out of Angelina and it would all be over. What on earth was Liam thinking about?

"Get on out of here with you, tinker. I got a real dislike for you and your kind," the sheriff growled.

Liam didn't bother answering, just clucked softly to the mules.

Reed couldn't remember the last time he felt so tense. His palms were slippery with sweat. His neck felt as if a thousand swamp mosquitoes were feasting on his hide and yet there wasn't one near him. His heart raced. He strained his ears and picked up the soft sounds of Angelina nursing.

"Had you scared there, didn't I, son?" Liam chuckled when they were on the outskirts of Ridgeland.

"Terrified," Reed said.

"Didn't want that sorry lawman to be thinkin' I was hidin' something. If I'd been all scared and ready to run, he'd of gone off somewhere and thought about it awhile, then he would've come lookin' for me. Way it is, I made him mad and he'll hate me but he don't have any idea Geneva is back there. 'Sides I heard that baby nursin' and knowed she would be quiet," Liam said.

"Reed?" Geneva's voice was barely a whisper on the evening breeze.

"We're outside town and—" Reed said softly.

"And goin' to stop right soon. We'll make dinner over an open fire and sleep under the stars, the tinker way," Liam said. "And you two got some talkin' to do."

Liam shaved bacon into a heavy black skillet, added an onion and potatoes sliced very thin. While that cooked, he opened two cans of beans. Geneva sat back away from the fire with Angelina and Reed gathered more sticks to keep the fire going.

"Okay, now it's cooking. Tell me what is going on," Liam said. "I knew your family, Geneva. I've known you since the day you were born. Thought for a while you'd be my daughter-in-law, but Rudy couldn't get past the idea you was taller'n him. Sylvie was your best friend growin' up. You didn't kill that husband of yours and I know it."

"No, I didn't," Geneva said. "I hid in the cellar. They came for me, not him. There's an ex-slave, Mazell, who came to clean the house for Hiriam. We became friends. The men in the white robes and hoods hung her husband. They said it was for making advances toward a white woman, but Mazell said it was because he was having meetings to encourage the black folks to vote when the time came. I went to her house and helped her during the funeral, cooking and serving and all. They came to hang me for that but I hid. They hung Hiriam because they couldn't find me, then they burned down the house while I was in the cellar. I walked to town and got on the stage to Ridgeland. I'm going to Lynchburg to my aunt's house." She told the story as if she were reciting a dull poem.

"And you?" Liam turned to Reed.

"Me, I'm a Yankee soldier sent down here to help with reconstruction. It's been a nightmare. I'm on my way home to Pennsylvania, Love's Valley to be exact. I got on the stage with Geneva. The drivers robbed the stage. Tossed us out on the side of the road and this ex-slave woman offered us the use of her house. I didn't even know Geneva was having a baby until it was almost born. I just thought she was fat," Reed said.

The chuckle started deep in Liam's chest and

erupted into a full fledged howl that had him fetching his handkerchief from the pocket of his bibbed overalls. "Did you tell her that?" Liam wiped at his eyes and hiccupped.

"Yes, he did, and I really don't see what is so funny," Geneva cocked her head to one side, the flickering fire flashing in the anger of her blue eyes.

"You, fat. That's what's so funny. That and no woman likes to be told she's fat. That's a dirty word according to my Sylvie. She says even after six children that Luke better never call her fat," Liam continued to wipe at his eyes.

"Well, she was fat, and dirty too," Reed said.

"And with those words you have just proven what a stupid Yankee you are," Liam said. "Now don't go getting your dander up none. A Southern gentleman would never have said those two words even if he did think them, and one of the Tuatha'an would have been careful not to even think them. That wagon is our home for several months out of the year. We don't have a big fine house with many rooms to get away from the wife so we are careful what we think and even more careful what we say. How'd you like to be caged up in that wagon in a raging thunderstorm with an angry woman after you'd called her fat and dirty? You have many lessons to learn, Yank," Liam told him.

"I see that," Reed finally grinned. "But I have no intentions of having a wife, either in a wagon or a big fine house for many years."

"And I have no intentions of ever having another husband," Geneva declared vehemently.

"And I was about to suggest that maybe you would marry me," Liam's old eyes twinkled. "My wife has been gone on long enough now that I feel safe that her ghost isn't going to claw its way up from the grave like she said she would if I ever looked at another woman. Sylvie has her own husband and children. Rudy is married and doing well with his tinker wagon. You could use a husband and a wagon. I could use someone to cook for me and a baby to keep me entertained."

Reed held his breath. Surely Liam was joking. Surely Geneva wouldn't take him seriously, and yet, if she did, he'd be rid of the responsibility. He would be released from his word to take her to Lynchburg and he could accept it in all honesty.

"You are kidding, Liam, and even if you weren't the answer would be no," Geneva said. "I will never marry again. I'm going far away so the Sheriff of Savannah can never find me and so I can make a life for Angelina and me. We don't need a man to tell us what to do and when to do it."

"Never say never, my child," Liam stirred the potatoes and beans. "Of course, I am joking with you. A young woman like you would have no truck with an old tinker like me. Besides I did not bury my wife face down and it is possible she would claw her way up to haunt me if I married again. A few words of advice from an old man, though: I will take you to the stage station in Ridgeland in the middle of the morning tomorrow. Reed says the sheriff is leaving at first light. Go on the stage as Mr. and Mrs. Reed Hamilton and travel that way until you get to Lynchburg to your aunt's house. You can pretend and it will cover your tracks. You might even learn to call her Genny instead of Geneva, Reed. The sheriff must be pretty sure she knew who was hiding under those sheets and pillow-cases and if she starts talking about it, he will be in trouble. The unrest in the South is as bad as the war. Geneva has no business in that part of the land even if things could be made right. Take her to Lynchburg. She can start all over there."

"Sounds like good advice," Reed said, swallowing hard at even pretending to be married to the woman for a few days until they reached Lynchburg.

"It doesn't to me," Geneva said. "It sounds like men telling me what to do again. I've had enough of it. When we get to the stage station tomorrow, I'll go under my maiden name, Geneva O'Grady."

"To be sure, you should do just that. I'm quite sure the sheriff has already figured out such a simple thing, Genny," Liam used the name he'd called her when she was a child playing with his young Sylvia, who was still known as Sylvie.

Geneva stewed about the idea the entire time she ate supper. Hot fried potatoes, skillet biscuits and gravy made from a quart of milk Liam miraculously pulled from the back of the wagon. She left the beans for the men to eat since she did not want a colicky baby in the night. What Liam had suggested made perfect sense but she didn't want to even pretend to be a wife again. He said to never say never. But she was not only saying never, she was screaming it. They could take up a big, flat river rock, engrave *never* on the stone and keep it to the day of her death to be used as a tombstone. She would never marry again. Her father was dead so he couldn't lose her in a card game. No man would ever own Geneva again.

"You and the baby can take the cot inside the wagon," Liam said after they'd eaten in silence. "Reed and I can make do out here under the stars."

"Thank you," Geneva held Angelina in the sling and begrudgingly let Reed help her up into the back of the wagon. "And thank you for your help, Mr. Hamilton. I am grateful, but Angelina and I will be fine on our own."

Reed nodded. He sincerely hoped they would. But something deep down in his gut told him this game hadn't been played to the end and things could change even yet.

"She'll change her mind, you know," Liam said softly after they'd chosen their places to bed down. "She's a stubborn lass, has been since the day she was born. But she's also sensible. She'll see it's the only way. I'll go on into town tomorrow about mid-morning and buy two tickets. Of course you will give me money to buy them. I'll put down that they are for a married couple and use your name. The stage man won't ever see you so he'll think it's for an old man and his wife. Then I'll come back here with the tickets and we'll stop the stage on its way to Pocotaligo and board the both of you. It'll take all day to get there. You can tell her on the way what I did, but please wait until I'm far away. She might not be a full-blooded tinker seeing as how her mother was a Southern belle from Virginia, but she's got enough wild tinker blood in her to pitch a hissy fit. I'd as soon be far away when she finds out."

"You got my word," Reed said quietly. "You think Pocotaligo is far enough away that she could go on her own from there?"

"No, I'd manage to keep her married until Lynchburg. I worry that the long arm of that evil sheriff might even reach that far," Liam said.

"Whew!" Reed exhaled.

"Might trying, these women folks," Liam said.

Before Reed could answer, he heard Liam snoring loudly.

Geneva heard the tones of quiet talk but couldn't make out the words. It didn't matter what they said, she was having her way this time. Come hell, high water, or even another war, she wasn't going to pretend a marriage to anyone—most especially a Yankee.

Chapter Seven

The stagecoach driver eyed Geneva as Reed helped her into the coach. They'd been expecting an older couple according to what the station manager had said. The sheriff from Savannah, Georgia, had left a description of a tall, good-looking, blond woman in the family way that they needed to be on the lookout for. Even though the couple wasn't elderly by any means, the woman couldn't be the one the sheriff described either. He'd said she was a tall beauty and the woman was tall but not very good-looking. The driver cocked his head off to one side and squinted. No, nothing that could be called a beauty there. Her eyes were pretty but the rest of her just looked like an oversized woman that most men would run a country mile to get away from. No, she and her husband were nothing more than Georgia crackers or South Carolina swamp rats. That they had enough money to buy passage all the way to Pocotaligo was the only surprise they had in store for the driver. It was impossible to fathom her as a plantation owner's fancy Southern wife, not with a sling like that holding a baby in it. Rich women hired nannies to carry their babies for them. They sure didn't put them in a sling like a slave woman going out to pick cotton.

"I'd reckon you two won't mind riding way up past dark. There'd be a basket of food in the floor. Old feller that bought your tickets said you might be needin' victuals along the way since we don't stop at any stations so he paid for your dinner and supper. If you got an emergency that requires a bush to hide behind, rap on the door right loud. Other than that, we'll only stop every three hours for fifteen minutes to give the horses a rest. Got any questions, either one of you?" The tall, lanky man hitched the gun belt a little higher on his hip as he talked.

Geneva shook her head. Reed did the same.

"Sheriff of Savannah, Georgia, back there said to be on the lookout for a big tall blond haired woman name of Geneva Garner. Said she was quite the looker. Just so I can say I asked, ma'am, and since you are a tall woman with what looks to be straw colored hair peeking out around that bonnet, what is your name?" He blushed and looked down at the ground.

"Her name is Genny Hamilton. She's my wife. Why would the sheriff from Savannah be looking for a woman anyway?" Reed asked, weathering the snowstorm blasting from Geneva's eyes very well, or so he thought.

"Said she murdered her husband and burned down his house. Me, I thought Sherman had took care of all the plantation houses in these parts, but I guess him and this woman's husband got along well enough, he didn't burn his place down. Wife did it for him," the man said. "Glad it ain't you, though. I knowed you two was just a couple of plain old poor people. But I had to ask just to be sure. What are you goin' off to Pocotaligo for?"

"To see my wife's aunt and maybe hustle up some work," Reed said.

"Well, good luck, son. Ain't no jobs anywhere in the south. Not unless you'd be one of them reconstruction men from the north. Southern men ain't got the rights that even slaves has got right now. Good day to you both. We'll try right hard not to hit too many holes and wake the baby, ma'am," he tipped his hat and in a few minutes the stage began to roll north.

"I told you I wasn't playing that game," Geneva hissed between clenched teeth.

"Then rap on the door and tell those two your real name and go on back to Savannah to face the bogus charges against you. Would you like me to take Angelina on to your aunt's house so she can raise her? I don't think they take too kindly to babies in jail-houses while they're building a gallows," Reed shot right back at her.

Geneva snapped her mouth shut but her eyes gave away her rage. If looks could kill, Harry Reed Hamilton's cold dead body would have flown out the window of the stage to land in a pile of fresh horse manure. They rode the entire rest of the day in total silence, not even speaking when they had fifteen minutes of time to walk about and stretch their legs. If Geneva would have had the choice to talk to that impossible Yankee or die, they'd have to start fitting her for an extra long coffin. If Reed ever got to Lynchburg with his sanity, he would indeed believe in pure miracles.

Luck was with them that night. The hotel had two rooms available with a connecting door. The desk clerk called it the honeymoon suite. One room was for the groom; the other for the bride. Geneva dragged herself and the baby up the stairs, weary from the long ride, hungry, and ready to do battle with Reed if he so much as turned the handle on the connecting door. The desk clerk yelled for a kid named Jim Bob to carry Reed's trunk up the stairs.

"I'd like a tub of water brought to both rooms tonight," Reed said. "Lots of hot water for my wife," he almost choked on the words.

"That'll cost you extra," the clerk eyed the poor man's clothing.

"Cost is not an issue," Reed said, pulling several bills from his pocket and laying them on the counter. "I also want a good hot supper delivered to my wife's room and to mine also. Just as soon as it can be rustled up. And would you be so kind as to send a message to the owner of the general store. I'm aware that it is well past his closing time, but my wife is in need of a few things. I will make it worth his while to come to my room within the next fifteen minutes."

"Yes, sir," the desk clerk picked up the bills and smiled brightly. "I will arrange everything for you."

"Thank you," Reed said stiffly and started up the stairs. Why, oh why, he berated himself, hadn't he sailed and suffered with sea sickness? If he'd only bought passage on a ship, he'd be more than halfway home by now. Perhaps a little green around the upper lip and a few pounds lighter, but without a woman and child in his care.

Geneva took Angelina from the sling and laid her in the middle of a big feather bed. She dropped a smelly pillowcase of soiled nappies and baby clothing on the floor. At least there was a wash basin on the stand beside the bed. She dampened a cloth in the cool water and and ran it over her face and neck, amazed at how much dust and dirt remained on the white cloth when she finished. She'd have to ask for more water. What was in the basin would never do the laundry. As late as it was already, she only hoped it would dry by morning.

Covered in a patchwork quilt, the bed took up most of the room. The wash stand, a rocking chair, and a small vanity with a round mirror finished up the furniture. Geneva paced around the bed, her stomach growling. Dinner had been a chunk of yellow cheese and a quarter loaf of bread. Supper had been more of the same. It had kept body and soul stuck together but it left a lot to be desired when everything she ate went to milk for Angelina.

She stopped long enough to check her reflection in the mirror. Her face had never been so gaunt or pale. Her waistline was still heavy from the baby but it was gradually getting smaller. She'd roped in the baggy dress she'd worn those last days of her pregnancy with a belt she'd found in the trunk at the plantation. All in all, she looked like something the dogs dragged in and the cats wouldn't have. No wonder the stagecoach driver didn't think she could be a tall good-looking woman. She looked an absolute fright.

The image in the mirror jumped when someone knocked on the door. She started across the floor to give Reed Hamilton a healthy dose of her anger when she realized the knock wasn't on the door between their rooms but from the outside. Holding her breath for fear she'd find the Savannah sheriff on the other side, she eased the door open a crack and peeped out.

"Mrs. Hamilton, ma'am, your husband has ordered that I bring your supper to you. If you will open the door, I'll bring the table inside," a big, strapping boy said.

She opened the door full wide and stood agog while the boy lifted a small table and carried it inside the room. He dragged the chair from in front of the vanity and placed it on one side of the table.

"Thank you," she murmured, hardly able to take her eyes from the food. A rich bowl of potato soup, roast beef in gravy surrounded by potatoes and carrots, enormous slices of bread slathered with butter, and a china pot of steaming hot tea.

"Oh, and your bath will be arriving in fifteen minutes. If you ain't done with your meal, we'll just put the tub inside the door and fill it while you eat. It'll take more than one trip to bring up all the hot water anyway," he said and disappeared out the door.

"Oh, my," she mumbled as she crammed first a bite of bread dipped in the soup, then a piece of carrot in her mouth. It was absolutely wonderful and she intended not to waste one single morsel.

Suddenly the door between the rooms flew open and was filled with Reed Hamilton's presence. It was as if he were more than a mere man standing there; as if he were a force. "Your bath will be here shortly. I would like to tell you that you could wallow in the water until you are as dried up as a prune, but you won't have time. The owner of the general store will be arriving in an hour with anything he has in ready-made women's clothing that might fit you. He's already been here and I've told him how big you are."

Before she could say a word, even to thank him for the lovely meal, he was gone, the door firmly shut and the bolt on the other side thrown. Obvious that he didn't want her to come waltzing into his room like he'd just done hers. Just went to show that she was right. Men could do whatever they wanted and women had to endure it. But women didn't have the same rights. However, if Reed thought for one minute he'd won that battle he was in for one big surprise, *How big she was!* Evidently Reed Hamilton had just as much trouble with her height that Rudy had had when she was a teenager. She'd never understand why men thought women had to be whimpering little rosebuds.

"A bath," she almost swooned, forgetting the issue of short, tall, big, small or even pretty and ugly. One she could sit in even if it wasn't until she was as wrinkled as a prune. And then she could use the water for laundry. She made herself eat slower and enjoy the food.

She'd finished bathing and put her baggy dress and belt back on when the rap on the door came letting her know the store owner had arrived. She cracked the door to find a woman even taller than she was staring back at her. "Yes, can I help you?" she asked.

"I'm Imogene Carson. My husband and I own the general store. You'd be Mrs. Reed Hamilton in need of a few things, I'd suppose?" she asked.

Heaven couldn't be better than this night, Geneva thought. The only black spot in the whole situation was having to stand there in her torn, ratty old dress made for the last month of pregnancy and admit she was Mrs. Reed Hamilton.

"Yes, I am and yes, I do. My things were destroyed in a fire," she said honestly.

The woman brought in three dresses, a navy blue traveling suit trimmed in black lace, two fashionable hats, and two lovely lawn nightgowns with robes to match and a whole array of undergarments, plus a trunk to keep them all inside. "Your husband told mine that you were tall but slender so I brought things I'd ordered ready-made for me. You can pick and choose among them and I'll order more tomorrow. Your husband said to tell you that you can have them all if you'd like. Y'all must be havin' an argument for me to be relayin' the messages. Ain't uncommon for husbands and wives to argue right after the first baby comes. Husbands don't understand the moods us women folk go through with birthin'. They try but they're just men and bein' such they think with the wrong side of their brains."

"I couldn't take them all," Geneva was settling on one dress, the light blue one and the traveling suit. Both had buttons up the front and would work fine for nursing Angelina on the long trip.

"Yes, you can," Reed opened the door again. "She will have all of them and we thank you for your time and efforts after normal hours. I will recompense you for both."

Geneva gritted her teeth, unable to say a word to the abominable Yankee right there in front of the woman. When they got to Lynchburg, she'd beg her aunt for the money to reimburse him every single penny he'd spent. She would never be beholden to a man, especially a Yankee.

"The bill then," the lady handed him a handwritten piece of paper.

He pulled a roll of bills from his pocket and peeled off several. "Thank you once again. Genny and I will be leaving first thing in the morning. The stage for Ridgeland leaves at daybreak I'm told."

"So that's where you're headed. Some reason I figured you were going north," she tucked the money into her pocket. "That stage, the one for Walterboro leaves at the same time. I, for one, never see either of them. Got six kids I'm trying to feed and get ready to send off to school at that time of the morning. Good night to you both then, and thank you for your business. A little word of advice from a woman who's birthed six critters like that one layin' on the bed over there: Don't stay mad at each other forever. It wears on you and makes a bigger hurt than the one that's already there. Just call it a meddling old mother who doesn't like to see young couples at odds with one another," she grinned and shut the door behind her, leaving them both in awkward silence.

"I shall repay you as soon as we get to Lynchburg," Geneva said stiffly.

Angelina set up a howl before Reed could tell her she didn't owe him a thing. She had no idea what the Hamilton family was worth, or what Reed had amassed of his own fortune. A smile tickled the corners of his mouth as he thought about that. No end of women in the Love's Valley area had set their caps for one of the Hamilton boys even before the war. They'd seen a prosperous farm and a bank account big enough to choke a good-sized steer and the young Hamilton men had had their work cut out for them just keeping ahead of the race. Then the war came and they'd all gone off to do their duty. Two of his brothers were now married to Southern women. He wondered as he watched Geneva try to comfort her daughter if deep down she'd married Hiriam Garner because she saw dollar signs when she looked at him.

"Hush, baby girl," Geneva crooned and Angelina cried even harder.

"Give her to me," Reed reached out. "You can pack your things in the trunk and I'll rock her."

"She's crying," Geneva drew back.

"So she'll cry with me instead of you. If you get all that folderol put in the trunk right now, then it will be ready to go early in the morning. I don't want to miss that stage and have to stay here another day," he motioned with his fingers for her to let him have the baby.

The minute she laid Angelina in his arms, the baby stopped crying and looked up at him intensely only the way a new baby can do. A tiny invisible string moved from her little heart to wrap itself firmly around his, tugging gently to unite the two of them. He sat down in the rocking chair without breaking the stare they shared, and began rocking gently back and forth the way he'd seen his dad do when Indigo was born.

"Why did you tell that woman we were going to Ridgeland?" she asked, turning her back as she folded drawers and camisoles to pack them back in the trunk. She'd never had such fine undergarments, not even when she was first married to Hiriam. He'd bought her common muslin and calico from the general store and told her to make her own things when she was first sure about the baby. Until then she'd worn what she'd had that fatal night when her father had lost her in the card game.

"Never know how far the long arm of that vengeful sheriff might reach," Reed said. "It might buy us a couple of days if it gets this far. If he puts a bounty on your head there'll be people hunting for you."

"I can't believe she's stopped crying," Geneva picked up a hat and placed it on her head, checking the reflection in the mirror.

"She knows who her—" Reed stopped mid-sentence. He'd almost said exactly what he'd heard his father say when he was rocking Indigo; something he'd said many, many times, "She knows who her daddy is."

"Who what?" Geneva laid the hat on the vanity. She'd wear it with the traveling suit tomorrow.

"Nothing," Reed touched Angelina's small hand and instantly her fingers wrapped around his thumb. "Pocotaligo was the first place I saw fighting in the war," he said, looking into the baby's sweet face.

"Oh? I'm going to do the day's laundry if you don't mind rocking her awhile longer," Geneva dumped the pillowcase of soiled baby clothes into the tub of water. "I asked the boy who brought the water if he'd set a couple of buckets of cold water outside the door for me to use as rinsing water. Maybe I can get it all done before she sets up a fit to be fed."

"I don't mind," Reed said, the rocking motion relaxing him as much as it did the baby.

"Want to talk about it? The war, I mean. What happened here in this town?" She asked as she opened the door just as the young man was coming up the stairs, a bucket in each hand. "If you'll bring them inside," she motioned toward the tub.

"Do better than that, ma'am," Jim Bob said. "Mr. Hamilton's tub has been emptied. I'll just bring it through the door and fill it up for you. That'll make the job easier. Oh, and I brought up a length of rope. We get families who need to do washin' all the time. I'll string up a line over in Mr. Hamilton's room. If he leaves the window open then this heat will have it dried by mornin'."

"I thank you," Geneva smiled brightly and Jim Bob blushed scarlet.

Reed almost hummed as he rocked. For a moment there was peace in the hotel room. Peace that he never thought he'd find anywhere, most of all in Pocotaligo, South Carolina, the place where he'd found out just what war was all about. Someday, he promised himself as he sat there, babe in arms, he was going to have a whole yard full of children. No wonder his father enjoyed rocking Indigo so much. It wasn't so much as to quiet the baby but rather his own soul.

"So you were going to tell me all about this place," Geneva said as she began the wash.

Reed had never told anyone about that first year in the war. Not even his brothers when they'd met at the farm after the war and had soon been dispersed in three different directions to help with the reconstruction of Texas, Louisiana, and Georgia. He wasn't sure he wanted to share it, but telling Geneva would get it off his chest. Maybe if he told her he'd leave behind the nightmares and the memories in Lynchburg when he said good-bye to her and Angelina.

"I came down here a green kid who thought war was like a big game. At first we figured we'd whip those Southern boys into shape in a few weeks, go home heroes and all that. It didn't happen like that. We got into Pocotaligo in the middle of August. I hadn't sat down to a dining room table in months, but a few of us were invited to sit with the captain in a Southern home on the outskirts of town. One of those Sherman burned later on, I'm sure. It was a humbling experience just sitting there with a glass to drink cool water from. Things I'd taken for granted my whole life and done without forever, or so it seemed.

"Anyway, on September 8 of that year there was a tug named the *Daffodil* that towed twenty-six of the boats in the assault on Fort Sumter. I was on that tug, helping with the towing, when I found out I can't abide ships. The minute one of my feet leaves solid ground, I turn green and begin to gag. It's a good thing there wasn't anything on my stomach that cool fall day when the fighting started, though, so maybe I shouldn't begrudge the experience.

"The battle began on October 22. On our side there were forty-three killed, nearly three hundred maimed and injured, and three captured. My friend was the doctor and I helped him all night with the injured. Not that I had one bit of medical experience, but I was a scout. Folks said I could smell a two-week-old footprint, but they used me wherever I was needed when I wasn't out looking for Rebel track. Mitch, my friend, would sometimes ask me to help him so the other doctors could do their jobs. I saw both Southern and Northern boys lying on the ground, their blood mingled together as it flowed into the Carolina dirt, and I wondered what in the hell I was doing here. Some of the bullet holes in those kids . . . I'd fired the gun that put them there.

"Those boys weren't going home to sit at a dining room table with their families ever again. They believed in what they were fighting for just as much as I did. So much that they'd died for it. I asked myself if I would die for my beliefs, not that it mattered one whit. I was knee-deep in the war that wasn't going to be over in a few months. I faced the fact I'd most likely end up with my blood flowing into some southern dirt, but deep down in my heart did I believe that strongly? I asked myself that question a million times, more than once a day, and I did my duty, but I never did get an answer. One minute I'd be convinced I could stand in front of a firing squad of raging Rebels and go to eternity a hero. The next I just wanted to go home and forget the whole thing, be branded a coward if necessary.

"It all seemed so useless. Fighting. Tearing apart a country. Ripping apart families. Lifetimes of hard work all wetting down the soil with blood. Another lifetime to rebuild what both sides demolished during those years," he kept his eyes on the baby's unwavering stare as he spoke. Almost as if he were begging a baby less than two weeks old to understand how he felt.

"I understand," Geneva hung up the last of the nappies on the line Jim Bob had stretched in the other room. "There are lots of things that happen in a lifetime to bring us to our senses and make us realize how much we take for granted. Looks like she's been good long enough for me to finish. It'll be an early morning for us both, Reed. We'd better try for some sleep. That stage won't give us much comfort."

"Thanks for listening, Genny," he said softly as he reluctantly handed Angelina over into her mother's care.

"Thanks for trusting me enough to tell it," she said.

He shut the door but this time she didn't hear the bolt lock.

Chapter Eight

Tension was thick on the streets of Walterboro that
night when the stage pulled up in front of a hotel and
stage station combined. The air was still, sultry, as if
the breeze waited on the outskirts to see what would
happen before it swept down the streets. Where there
should have been a tinkling piano from the saloon
next door, a deadly silence prevailed, making the hair
on Reed's neck stand straight up. Something definitely was wrong, yet, other than the eerie quiet, nothing
appeared out of place. Still, Reed felt like he did just
before the start of a battle. Those first few minutes of
uncanny silence and then all hell would break loose.

Geneva didn't like the feeling Reed's hand on her
elbow evoked when she got out of the stage. They'd
been quiet most of the trip and Reed had even slept,
snuggled down into the corner of the coach, but she'd
been too antsy to sleep. Reed had mentioned that the

sheriff might go so far as to send a bounty hunter for her. Why would he do that, she'd pondered all day. Then the reason became clear. The sheriff himself wanted the land that Hiriam's plantation sat on. It bordered another piece of property he'd bought recently. Hiriam had had words about the sale, saying that before the war the sheriff wouldn't have been able to afford a two-acre mosquito ranch, let alone a plantation of that size. But he'd bought it for taxes. Now if Geneva and Angelina were both dead, Hiriam's place would go for taxes also. She shivered at the idea when she walked into the hotel. At least the town was a nice quiet one. No brawls going on out in the street. Not even the sounds of a piano from one of the saloons.

"What's goin' on?" the driver asked the desk clerk. "Sounds like the whole town died."

"Got a race problem," the man said. "Black man got radical in his newspaper about the white people blaming the black population for all the crimes around here. Bunch of them Klan people hung him this afternoon. Black folks are down at the church havin' a meetin' about it right now. Need a room?" the man looked up at Reed and Geneva.

"Couple," Reed said. The tension in Walterboro wasn't any worse than what he and Geneva had ridden in most of the day. They'd awakened to a strange, hurried awkwardness. Geneva, lovely in the new traveling suit; Reed, admiring her beauty, but not willing to comment on it. He'd slept or pretended sleep while he rode most of the day. He should never have told her his innermost feelings about the war.

"Got a couple right next door to each other," the man said. "Need someone to carry those trunks? Cost you extra. How about a bath or supper? That'd be extra too."

"Yes to all. We want supper served in our room and baths," Reed said, signing them in as a married couple and laying several bills on the desk.

"Jefferson," the man yelled toward the dining room.

An enormous black man appeared, his very size intimidating Geneva. He had to duck to get his head through the door and the scowl on his face left no doubt he'd rather be anywhere other than the hotel. "Yes, sir," he said in a deep-throated growl.

"Folks need their luggage toted up to their rooms. Number two and three right at the top of the stairs," the clerk said.

Jefferson snarled his nose and picked up a trunk, mumbling about rich whites thinking they could order common people around. Before he'd reached the bottom step the plate glass window in the front of the hotel exploded in a blast of glass. A screaming mass of black faces swirled into the lobby of the hotel. Jefferson threw the trunk onto the floor and joined his brothers in race as they grabbed the desk clerk and pushed him outside along with Reed and Geneva.

Reed reached for Geneva's hand and held it tightly as they were pushed along in a swarming crowd of faces. Jefferson was the leader, yelling that they need-ed to hang the three whites.

"An eye for an eye, a tooth for a tooth. If thy right hand offend thee, cut it off," he chanted, his eyes crazy as he incited the others to chant with him. "Cut it off! Cut it off! Cut it off!"

Fearful that Geneva and Angelina would be swept away from him or worse yet, that they would fall and be trampled to death, Reed hesitated before he let go of her hand, squeezing it first, he hoped reassuringly one more time.

Pure panic caused Geneva to grip Angelina so tight the baby set up a howl in the melee. White men wearing white sheets, hanging Hiriam. Angry black men about to hang her and Reed just because they were white. Had the war made monsters of every man left on the face of the earth?

Reed carefully reached into the shoulder holster under his jacket and removed his Colt. He fired it once straight up into the night air. Everything stopped. The noise, the movement. Two men closest to him reached out to grab the gun from him but he pointed it right at one's chest.

"I don't know what you are enraged about," he said calmly, every fiber in his being wanting to break and run, yet there was no way out of the dense crowd of anger, "but whatever it is, my wife and I had nothing to do with it. So unless you want to bury this man tomorrow morning, I suggest you make a nice big pathway and let us go right back to the hotel."

"You whites, you hung our leader, our newspaper man," Jefferson stormed right up next to Reed. "We don't care if you be from here or not. We just want to have our eye for an eye. I figure it'll take all three of you and this baby—" he wretched Angelina from

Geneva's hands, "—to make atonement for him. Cut it off. Cut it off," he started chanting again but no one joined him.

"Give me my child," Geneva said.

"Just a little white baby," Jefferson chuckled. "Don't need to be wasting a rope on the likes of a little baby. We'll just hold her nose shut until she stops breathing."

"Genny," Reed said and tossed her the gun in one fluid movement as he snatched Angelina from Jefferson's arms.

Geneva shoved the barrel of the gun into Jefferson's chest, right about where she figured his evil heart should be. "I can and will pull this trigger," she said, her finger itching. Angelina was howling in indignation and fright. Reed had saved her life again. That made twice in the baby's short lifetime. Once from a wild boar; once from a crazy man.

Jefferson's eyes gave away his horror. Most women would cower in his presence. Even one as tall and big as the man-sized lady in front of him, but her eyes held only disgust and rage. She wouldn't pull the trigger though. She was just a whimpering white woman even if she was a big one. Women didn't have the guts to kill. Jefferson's eyes softened as he reminded himself of that.

"I mean it. Call it off. Tell them to go home," she said.

"They'll rip you up into little pieces if I tell them to," he snarled at her, bravado filling his newfound confidence in knowing she was just a woman.

"And you'll be dead before they start," she said. "I think there are about six bullets in this gun. I'm a good shot. There will be six men lyin' dead before anyone has a chance to rip me to shreds."

The cold steel of the barrel caused a chill to shoot up his backbone. If he backed down now, he'd lose all respect. A veil fell over his eyes and he laughed. "You won't kill me. You might be a horse of a woman but you ain't got it in you to kill a man even if he's a black slave man. An eye for an eye," he intoned toward his silent followers, "a tooth for a tooth. Hangin's too good for these people. Kill 'em where they stand. Cut it off. Cut it off." With a huge hand the size of Geneva's head, Jefferson drew back to send the gun flying.

Geneva pulled the trigger and took a step back, avoiding the slap that could have broken her wrist. As the man fell to his feet and then face forward on the dusty main street of Walterboro, South Carolina, she spun around, looked over the crowd and pointed her gun at the closest man. "Who's next to die?" she asked in a soft Southern voice that left no doubt she meant business. "I've got five more bullets. Step right up and form a line or else I can just shoot at random. Who knows, I might get two for one that way. I didn't do one thing to you people. Neither did that desk clerk or my husband, most especially my baby. But I will kill however many I can before I let you harm a hair on my child's head."

A slow rumble began in the ranks and suddenly a pathway opened up in the crowd in the direction of the hotel. Arms that held the desk clerk relaxed. "You killed my brother," a man said from behind her. "You'll have to pay for that. An eye for an eye. Don't let her through. She won't shoot no body else."

She spun around and faced a man, not as big or intimidating as Jefferson, but one just as full of anger. "Is your Momma still livin'?" she asked him.

"Yes," he answered.

"Then she can bury two sons tomorrow if this doesn't cease right now," Geneva said.

"Shut up, Abraham," one of the other men said. "It's over. We wasn't doin' right no way. Just got caught up in the madness is all. Just because they hung our friend, don't give us no right to kill a baby and innocent folks. That makes us no better than them. We'll just have to figure out a way to put out our paper next week same as always. That will do more good and we'll tell in it how them Klan members have to hide because they know they're doin' wrong. Take Jefferson home and bury him."

"An eye for an eye," Abraham yelled, shaking his fist in the air.

"Give me my child," Geneva kept the gun trained on Abraham's chest. When Reed had put Angelina back into her arms, she carefully transferred the gun to his hands. "I'm going to the hotel and these two are going with me," she pointed at Reed and the desk clerk. "If one of you so much as touches the sleeve of my garment, Mr. Hamilton is going to shoot you."

With that she marched down the road, dirt kicking up in dust devils around her skirt tails. When she got back to the hotel lobby, she turned with a glare to the desk clerk. "I want my trunk brought upstairs. Since your errand boy is now dead, I suggest you bring it yourself. I'm also still going to want supper and a bath. I intend to lock the door to my room and if you want inside you need to identify yourself. I feel certain Mr. Hamilton has another gun which I intend to sleep with tonight."

"Yes, ma'am," he said meekly. "And thank you for saving my life."

Geneva didn't even answer as she swept her full skirts aside and carried her weeping baby up the stairs. When the man had set her trunk inside her door and left, she slammed the door shut with enough force to rattle the windows, locked it, and melted into the rocking chair in the corner. Great God in heaven, she'd just murdered a man. She'd pulled the trigger without flinching and watched him die without an ounce of remorse. She needed to go to confession more than she'd ever needed to and yet, other than an intense shaking in her inner being, she felt less guilty over that than she did living with Hiriam a whole year without a marriage that could be recognized by the church.

"Hush now, baby," she crooned in a quivering voice. "Momma won't let anybody ever hurt you. It's all right now. We just proved we can take care of ourselves and we don't need a man to do it for us."

Reed stood in the lobby of the hotel in a stupor. Had he just awakened from a terrible nightmare or had Geneva really just killed a man? If she could kill like that without even blinking an eye, could he really believe her story about the Klan killing her husband? Or was it just a story she'd fabricated?

"Cedric?" A voice behind him made him jump and point the gun in that direction.

"It's all right, Mr. Hamilton," the desk clerk said from halfway up the stairs. "This is the sheriff of Walterboro. Sheriff, this man and his wife just stopped the riot. What on earth happened to set it off?"

"I might ask you the same thing," the sheriff said. "Put that gun away. It's breaking up out there. They're all going back home."

"I'll tell you what happened," Cedric said. He related the story, leaving out no detail, embellishing it very little. He actually shuddered when he told how Jefferson had grabbed and threatened to kill the baby and when he demanded the rioters tear them apart.

"That the way you saw it go down?" the sheriff asked Reed.

"Yes, sir, that's what happened. We'd just come into the lobby and gotten rooms when the noise started and Jefferson started yelling about an eye for an eye, and chanting the words, 'Cut it off. Cut it off.' Had the whole mass of them worked up in a frenzy. I believe they would have hung all of us or else ripped us to shreds with their bare hands. Will we be safe in this town tonight? We'll be on the first stage out of here to Cottageville come morning," Reed said.

"I'll send a deputy over to stand guard outside your room all night," the sheriff said. "Your wife is one brave woman, Mr. Hamilton. She's stopped a riot that could have resulted in a lot more deaths and a lot more property damage. A few storefronts have to be replaced but there was no looting like in that riot I read about down in Louisiana."

"Guess it doesn't pay to mess with a lioness' cub," Reed managed a weak smile. "I'd appreciate the deputy, sir. And Cedric, I do think my wife and I will share a room after all. She may be a bit more shook up than she appeared at first."

"Didn't look like it to me," Cedric said. "I'll fix up a couple of plates and bring them right away. Anything else breaks out tonight and I might be joinin' you in that room," he attempted a joke but it fell flat in the room.

"We'll be on patrol. I got a bunch of volunteers for the night," the sheriff said. "Tell your wife thank you for me."

"I will," Reed said, hoisting his own trunk on his shoulders and disappearing up the steep staircase.

He dropped it with a heavy thud right outside Geneva's door then knocked just as heavily. "Geneva, it's me, Reed. Please open the door."

He heard her footsteps on the wooden floor, softened at times by the rugs thrown on the floor, then the door opened. She still held Angelina in her arms, her eyes betraying the confidence her of her body.

"Are you all right?" he asked.

"Are they going to put me in jail for shooting that man?" she asked right back, blocking his way into the room.

"No. The sheriff said to send his thanks to you for stopping a riot that could have leveled the whole town," he told her. "I'm glad to see two beds. I was dreading sleeping on the floor and I told the desk clerk we'd only need one room. If there's trouble again, I want to be near you and Angelina."

"Why? To protect me? I can take care of myself," she said, her lower jaw beginning to quiver slightly and tears welling up in her eyes.

"Of course you can, but did you ever think maybe I want you to protect me?" he said lightly, kicking his trunk into the room with his foot, the scraping noise across the floor sending Angelina into another set of howls.

"I'm not sleeping in the same room with you," she declared. Though inside the quaking mess called her heart, she was glad to have him near. Glad that she wouldn't have to lie awake and worry all night whether that big man, Abraham, would kick down her door and smother her child. He'd said she would pay for killing his brother and he had to be smart enough to know she'd be on the next stage out of Walterboro.

"Then you stay awake all night," Reed said. "I'm sleeping in that bed. We can string up our laundry rope between the beds and separate the room if that makes you feel any better. Supper will be here in a few minutes," he carefully drew back the curtain over the window, staring down on the street. The sheriff was talking to a cluster of maybe five or six black men outside the saloon on the other side of the street. One of them kept pointing toward the hotel and gesturing with his hands. It looked like Abraham was still protesting his brother's killing.

"Shhhh," she patted the baby's back. "It's all right, now, baby girl. It's all right. We'll be fine."

Reed wished he could promise her the same. He was still watching the fracas when the desk clerk knocked timidly on the door and identified himself immediately. Reed had his pistol back in his hand and pointed toward the door when Geneva opened it. He lowered it carefully when he realized it was indeed Cedric bearing a small table laden down with food.

"The deputy is downstairs having his supper. He'll watch the stairs until he's ready for bed then he will shake out a bedroll right across your doorway. You'll be safe for the night and the sheriff has already talked to the stage manager. You have tickets on the six o'clock stage to Cottageville," Cedric told them seriously. "Maybe by tomorrow afternoon all the tension will die down. It's been building for a couple of weeks. Y'all just got caught up in the middle of it."

Geneva didn't think she could put a single bite in her mouth, but she did anyway and between the two of them, they polished off a loaf of bread, two steaming bowls of beef stew, half a round of yellow cheese, and a whole apple pie.

"How can a person eat after they've taken a life?" she asked herself as much as Reed. "It seems unholy, somehow. I need a priest for confession."

"So did I after that battle at Pocotaligo. It was months before I got one though and more than one life had fallen by my hands by then too. What you did was self-defense. The man would have killed you and Angelina. Never doubt that. He was deranged, out of his mind. You are a strong woman," he said.

"No, I was just a cornered rat," she told him. "I'm glad Angelina is sleeping now. I checked all her fingers and toes and by the way she was hollering, I suppose everything is all right inside her. I don't think he hurt her by squeezing her too tight, did he?"

"No, I think she was just scared," Reed said.

"Bath water," Cedric called from the other side of the door.

"How are we going to manage that?" Geneva asked, longing for a hot bath to wash away the sin of killing.

"You can have the first one," Reed said. "I'll turn that rocker toward the window and keep a watch on what's going on out there. I can rock the baby while you bathe. Then you can do the same and we'll share the laundry duties if she goes to sleep. But don't expect to wash away the memories of killing that man, Geneva. I tried to do that after the battle at Pocotaligo. Went down to the cold river and stood in it for hours. It didn't work."

"What does?" she asked when Cedric had gone back for more water.

"Nothing. Time helps. But nothing ever makes it go away. Just find peace in the fact that there could have been a lot more than one dead person if you hadn't stopped the riot when you did," he said.

She nodded and handed him the baby. He turned the rocker toward the window and sat down, hoping to find peace again in rocking Angelina. After two more trips up the stairs, Cedric had the tub filled and Reed heard Geneva's clothing dropping in a heap on the floor.

Geneva sighed loudly when she sat down in the warm water. Reed was right. It washed the traveling dust away but it did not take away the hard knot of knowledge that she'd brought about a man's death. Reed was intelligent beyond his years, she'd give him that much. He understood what she felt—the numbness, the helplessness, the sheer weight of what she'd done. Someday she would find someone with the qualities that man possessed, hopefully. *No, I will not,* she sat up and began scrubbing her skin mercilessly with the rough wash cloth and lye soap. *I will not find someone like Reed. I don't want another husband to berate and belittle me. I just want to live my life as Angelina's mother. I've had a husband. I don't want another one.*

Chapter Nine

Geneva had nightmares again and was only half awake when she jumped out of bed. The flapping laundry that formed a wall between her bed and Reed's looked like the white clad figures in her dreams. She slapped at it, whimpering in her half-sleep, trying to shove aside the nightmare and find reality.

Reed had been up for more than an hour, sitting in the rocking chair, watching the orange sliver of sun peeking over the horizon. Geneva whimpered in her sleep, and then suddenly was beating the air around the clothing as if she were fighting a ghost. He was on his feet in minutes, his arms around her, drawing her to his chest. "It's all right. Wake up. You're just dreaming again, Genny. Wake up now," he said gently.

Her eyes snapped open and a shudder worked its way out from the core of her body. "Am I awake?" she whispered hoarsely.

"Yes, you are awake now. It was just a dream," Reed said, keeping her safe in his arms awhile longer until she stopped shaking.

"But it was so real," she leaned back enough to look up. His face was smooth from a fresh shave and there was a dot of blood right there on his sharp chin line. A few drops of water still hung in his dark hair and his light brown eyes stared right into hers.

"I know. They can be sometimes," he said softly.

One moment he held her stare; the next his lips brushed hers ever so gently. Then the kiss deepened into something more, his tongue tickling the edges of her soft lips. Her knees didn't want to hold her. Somewhere out there in the distance she heard a soft song being played on a harp. Conflicting emotions shot through her. She wanted to stay in his arms forever; she wanted to slap his handsome face. She wanted to analyze the trembling effects of a real kiss; she wanted to run away and never think of it again. Feelings screamed at her to make a sane decision about what she really wanted. She finally pulled away from him and abruptly turned her back, wrapping her arms around her waist, trying to still her storming heart.

"I'm sorry," he said.

"For what? For kissing a fat woman? For kissing a tinker's daughter? What are you sorry for, Reed Hamilton?" she asked breathlessly.

"For taking advantage of your nightmare. It just happened. I won't let it happen again," he said through clenched teeth, so angry at himself for lacking control that he could have very well put his pistol to his head and pulled the trigger.

"You don't have to worry about it happening again. Because I won't let it happen again. Now let's forget it and have Cedric take our trunks to the stage," she said with no warmth in her voice. She began to take the baby's things from the line and pack them in the trunk, saving out a valise full for travel.

"Babies should be kept at home and not traveled with until they're at least three years old," she mumbled the whole time she packed, glad that Reed had gone to find Cedric. "And my lips shouldn't be warm when my heart is so cold, either," she touched her freshly kissed lips and wondered if all kisses were supposed to be like that. Affecting a woman so much that her knees went weak and she wanted to melt into the man's arms. Hiriam's kisses grinding against her mouth never made her want to do anything but run away and hide.

"Breakfast will be served in ten minutes and then we'll go directly to the stage. The deputy will escort us just in case Abraham is lying in wait," Reed opened the door, his presence filling the room again like an intense force.

Geneva had changed into the traveling suit and was working with her hair at the small mirror hanging on the wall. Reed could scarcely believe that he'd ever seen her as a big, fat woman. She was beautiful beyond words with all that thick blond hair and those enormous blue eyes. Her pale complexion was only tainted by a few cute little freckles across her nose and even those were downright adorable.

"I'm almost ready," she said, hoping her voice didn't give away the way she really felt. "Maybe Angelina will sleep until we are underway."

"Perhaps," Reed managed.

"Excuse me," Cedric knocked gently on the door and then opened it. He carried a small table laden down with breakfast food. "The sheriff says to tell you that he and one of his deputies will be riding back behind the stage for a few miles just to be sure nothing happens right outside of town. Stage has to travel right through the area where the black community is."

"Thank you," Reed said seating Geneva and then himself. "We appreciate that. Breakfast looks good."

"We have a good cook here," Cedric said. "I'll have to replace Jefferson. He worked nights. Carrying and toting and helping with cleanup. I was afraid I'd lose the cook too. She's his aunty or some kind of kin. But she came right in this morning and went to work without a word. Y'all enjoy your breakfast now and I'll be up in a few minutes to carry down the luggage."

Geneva slathered butter on a biscuit and cut up two fried eggs. It still seemed odd to her she could eat a big meal after killing a man, or that she could swallow food after sharing a kiss like she'd just had with Reed. Nothing had made sense in the past year, though, so why should she expect it to make any now. At least by keeping her mouth filled she wouldn't be expected to talk.

An hour later they were safely aboard the coach without incident, the sheriff and his deputy following along behind them. The sheriff had eyed her carefully when he'd been introduced by Reed, asking her what her full name was since he'd had a telegram from Savannah to be on the lookout for a tall blond woman who was wanted for murder.

"Genny Hamilton," Reed said. "Strange thing is the sheriff was in Ridgeland when we went through there and asked the same questions. Guess there must be more than one tall blond-haired woman in these parts."

"Guess so," the sheriff said. "Just needed to ask though, to make sure she wasn't Geneva Garner or going by her maiden name, O'Grady. You hear of anyone like that, drop me a telegram. We don't take too kindly to a woman murdering her husband. According to the sheriff from down there, she's in the family way too. Woman out on the run in that shape. Mustn't have any shame about her at all," the sheriff said.

"I guess not," Reed had agreed.

Geneva bit the inside of her lip to keep from telling them all to drop dead. They would take the sheriff's word against hers because he was a man and she was just a woman. He could do the deed himself, wear his white flapping sheets and hoods, and yet the moment he uttered the word, she was guilty of the crime.

"Will I ever be really free?" she finally whispered to Reed.

"Yes, I'm taking papers to the President of the United States concerning the reconstruction in

Georgia. There's a report in there about the Ku Klux Klan and the way it's operating in that area. I will tell him your story, Genny. He was a personal friend of my father's and still is to my mother. I'm going to make him aware of that hornet's nest in Savannah and ask him to give me a paper exonerating you. You'll have to carry it with you so if there is trouble later, after the sheriff and his cohorts are investigated, you can show it to the authorities," he said.

"You'd do that for me?" she asked incredulously.

"It's what's right," he said simply. "I was hoping to purchase or beg for a few newspapers in Walterboro. Being the size town it is, surely they'd have a few old ones even if they didn't have the newer ones. Guess I'm in for another long, boring day."

Angelina started to fuss before Geneva could smart off about being sorry that riding with her was so boring. How could he change the subject so quickly anyway? One second they were talking about the very President of the United States and the next he's fretting because he doesn't have papers to read on the journey. Men! They all had one-track minds and most of the time it had to do with keeping them entertained and happy. She arranged a blanket over her shoulder and drew out a breast for the baby who latched onto it hungrily.

Another hour passed and the sheriff and his deputy rode right up beside the coach, rapped on the side beside the window and informed Reed that they were going back to town since everything seemed quiet. Reed thanked them for their care and waved them on.

"That should make you breathe easier," he told Geneva when they were gone.

"Yes, it does. But it's not fair that I should even have to worry about it, Reed. Why should I be on the run when I did nothing but hide in the cellar? Why isn't my word as good as that crooked lawman's? Just because I'm a woman and come from the tinkers doesn't make me a liar," she said.

"Ah, a thinking woman. Bet you think women ought to have the same rights as men and even vote," he said, hoping to draw her into a conversation that would pass the time of day. So far, she'd been mighty quiet on their stagecoach rides. Looking back she hadn't been much of a talker in the slave's cabins, either. Not at all like his sister, Indigo, who had an opinion about any and everything on the face of the earth, and wasn't one bit afraid to step right up and speak her mind. Or like his brother Monroe's wife, Adelida, who did the same. He wondered briefly while he waited on her to even answer just how in the world two strong-willed women like Indigo and Adelida were doing living under the same roof?

"Women are just as much human beings as men are," Geneva handed Angelina to Reed and nimbly rebuttoned her blue shirtwaist without removing the blanket. "Why shouldn't they have the same rights? And if the time ever comes when we can vote, I'll be the first in line to do so. They say ex-slaves will be able to vote soon. Don't you think it's strange that they will have more rights than women?"

"Not ex-slave women. Only the men will have voting rights," Reed held the sleeping baby loosely so he could look his fill of her delicate features.

"Only thing in the world more worthless than a white woman is a black one," Geneva told him. "It isn't right and it'll be a long time before it's made right, but if you took away the skirt tails we all have a similar mind, Reed. I think with my brain the same way you do so why couldn't I vote sensibly?"

"Women do not think the same as men. They think about taking care of a home, canning, raising babies, that sort of thing. Men think about finances, providing, protecting. Boys are reared differently than girls," he said.

"Then it needs to change. I'm going to think about all the things a mother does, those things you just said, and then I'm going to think about providing and protecting too. Because I'm never having to deal with a man in my house again," she said.

"That bad was it?" he asked, looking up and into the very depths of those crystal clear blue eyes.

"It's over," she said, reaching for Angelina.

"I'll hold her while she sleeps," he said. "Give your arms a rest. Has to be hard on your shoulders to hold her all day long."

"Thank you," she said and fell silent.

Conversation was over, leaving both of them to think whatever they wanted the rest of the day. Angelina awoke, was changed, fed, and slept again. The cycle repeated itself several times, the dirty laundry bag growing and smelling in the floorboard between them. About five miles out of Cottageville, they picked up another passenger. An elderly woman sitting on the side of the road with a valise.

"Whew," she said when she crawled into the coach. "I'd say there's a baby in here and been here most of the day."

"Yes, ma'am," Geneva nodded slightly.

"Well, it's only a few more miles to the station. Reckon I can bear up that long," she said. "How old is that kid?"

"Two and a half weeks," Geneva said.

"And you're traveling with it? You and your man crazy or what? You should be in the bed yet, lady. Why, in my day, we lay in for at least six weeks and didn't travel with a baby until it was trained. Other people didn't have to smell the dirty laundry that way," she said.

"It's a girl, not an *it,*" Geneva said. "And sometimes life doesn't hand out bowls full of cherries, it hands out lemons."

"Ain't it the truth," the woman nodded and went into a long tirade about her own health, her loss of her fortunes during the war, and so forth until Geneva wanted to borrow Reed's pistol and put an end to the constant chatter.

When they reached Cottageville, she was more than happy to get out of the stage and didn't even raise an eyebrow when Reed checked them into connecting rooms as man and wife. If he could get the President himself to sign a paper saying that she was not wanted for heinous crimes, then Geneva would pretend to be his wife until she had the papers in her hands. At least they would have their own rooms that night and she wouldn't find herself in his arms being kissed soundly the next morning.

By the time Reed made all the arrangements with the desk clerk and found his way up the stairs, Geneva was standing in front of the window staring out. She didn't even turn when he came into the room through the connecting door. The weight of the world rested on her shoulders; her head hung in what looked like shame and she'd wrapped her arms tightly around her waist. Angelina lay on the bed, kicking and flailing her little arms around, happy for the freedom.

"Want to talk about it?" Reed sat down on the edge of the bed beside the baby, letting her wrap her fingers around his thumb. Liking the way it felt.

"No," Geneva said. "It's over."

"You keep saying that but it won't be until you get it off your chest and face it. Kind of like being afraid of the water after you've nearly drowned. The only thing you can do is dive right back in and prove to yourself that you won't let the fear overcome you," he said.

"Are you saying I should think about marrying again?" she asked.

"I'm saying that whatever is eating at you is going to consume you if you don't talk about it. Way I figure it is, we got about another week or so in each other's company. Maybe a little more before we make it to Lynchburg. We'll get to a place soon where there's a railway and we'll make better time. After I deliver you into your aunt's hands and go on to Washington, I'll bring back the paperwork we talked about. Then you'll never see me again. So you can unload on me the way I did you about Pocotaligo. It'll be like telling your problems to the wind. We'll never be in each other's company so it will blow away," he said.

"See that church across the street. The white one with the bell tower? That's where I married Hiriam Garner. My father and I were living in a burned out plantation, not so very different from the one where Angelina was born. Cabins were a little nicer. We'd been there all winter, doing fine just the two of us. Daddy came into Cottageville on a Saturday to get supplies like he always did. I stayed back at the cabin. He'd come to be ashamed of me. Twenty-two-years-old and no one wanted me. Too tall. Too big. Too raw-boned. He used to say all those things. Also that I didn't know when to keep my mouth shut. At sixteen I was old enough to marry but I was already taller than all the young men. Liam's son Rudy liked me but he couldn't get past the height or the way the people would tease him if he did," she said.

"I'm sorry. I can't understand that way of thinking," he said.

She pulled up the rocking chair and sat down but didn't relax. Her eyes were filled with so much pain, Reed wanted to draw her into his embrace again and protect her. But he'd made her a promise that morning and he'd be hung from the bell tower on the church across the street if he broke it. After all, a man was only as good as his word.

"I'm sure you could if you were six inches shorter

than me," she said. "After all, men are men. That Saturday night he brought Hiriam back to the quarters with him. They'd gotten into a card game at the saloon and when the place closed down they wanted to play some more. I was already in bed but I heard them laughing and drinking more and more. At dawn, Daddy awoke me to tell me he'd lost me in a card game. He'd run out of money and used me to bet with. Hiriam had won me, fair and square, and was even going to marry me. He wanted a son to carry on his name and inherit his plantation. So Daddy told me to get myself ready to get married and to pack my belongings. Hiriam was taking me back to Savannah on the noon stage."

"Oh, my Lord," Reed whispered.

"My thinking exactly when I came out of the bedroom. Hiriam barely came to my shoulders. He was forty-nine-years-old and bald. He just sat there grinning like a cat who'd found a whole bed of mice. Daddy told me to accept my responsibilities and make the man a good wife, and to thank the stars that someone was finally willing to marry someone like me. Hiriam wasn't Catholic. He insisted that we marry in that church right there across the street. I never felt married to the man, not even after I knew Angelina was on the way. He told me every day that as soon as I produced a son he was kicking me out of his house. The church wouldn't recognize a marriage like that, Reed. So does that make my daughter illegitimate?"

"No, I wouldn't think so. I think any priest would grant you absolution for that. Good lord, there's not a

Father on the earth who wouldn't give you redemption from a situation like that," he said.

"What is redemption? Destiny is what decides the inevitable course of life and love, or so Momma said. Just what would you say redemption is, Reed? How would a priest redeem a whole wasted year?" she asked, finally looking up into his eyes.

"Redemption is blotting out the past," he said simply. "When we find a priest we'll both go to confession. We'll ask him to blot out the past so we can both have a sweeter future ahead of us."

"No man is capable of that," she said. "Not even a priest."

A knock on the door brought Reed to his feet. He opened the door wide to allow the steward to bring in a table with supper. Geneva left her rocking chair and joined him where they both ate in complete silence, enjoying the food, mulling over what they'd both revealed of their own pains and pasts. When they said their good-byes would this all really blow away into a redeemed past or would it stay with them forever?

Chapter Ten

There were no hotels the next night at Pump Pond. Just a stage station with a small dining room and no rooms to let. "The stage you come in on goes right back to Cottageville tonight and the next one north don't leave until day after tomorrow," the manager told them. "You and the missus there, you'd be welcome to throw a bed roll on the floor until then."

Geneva and Reed sighed in unison.

"Hey, Willard, you got any vittles cooked up. Thought we'd have us a hot meal 'fore we shove off," a man said as he and another came through the door.

"Got stew cooked and some beans should be ready 'bout now," Willard said. "You boys got that train loaded with wood and water already?"

"What train?" Reed asked.

"Oh, it ain't no passenger train," the taller of the

two men said. "Pump Pond is just a place where we take on water and wood so's we can make it the last leg of the journey up to Moncks Corner. Got to keep them steam engines happy. I'll have both, Willard. Bowl of stew and one of beans too. Got cornbread or apple pie?"

"Got cornbread but I fried up doughnuts today instead of making a pie," Willard told them.

"That's even better. By the way, I'm Simon the engineer and this here is Dale, my helper. We run the engines up and down this line every day. Good thing that Willard is a fine cook. We eat in here every day. Heard tell he was a cook in the South Carolina army durin' the war. He can fry the lightest doughnuts in the whole state." The man turned a wooden chair around backward and sat in it, propping his elbows on the back.

"How long does it take by train to get to Moncks Corner and is there a passenger train there?" Reed asked.

"Takes about two hours to get up there and yes there's a passenger train. But you'll have to wait a day or two for the stagecoach to come down here and get you. We don't take on passengers, just wood and water," Simon told him.

"Depends on if'n you'd want to ride in an empty train car," Dale said. "Wouldn't be comfortable, but it'd get you up there about midnight tonight. Cost you plenty."

"Can't do it, Dale," Simon said. "You know the

last time we let a man talk us into that we got in big trouble."

"Won't this time. We'd let them ride in that empty car that's goin' to bring lumber back down from Moncks Corner on the way to Savannah. They could give us the money for the ride and I'll make sure nobody sees them leaving the station," Dale said.

The way the man looked at her made Geneva's skin crawl worse than when the daddy longlegs paraded up and down her arms in the cellar of Hiriam's plantation house. Two days of sleeping on the floor and eating Willard's cooking didn't sound so ominous after all when she considered two hours of being at that man's mercy.

"How much?" Reed asked.

"Twenty dollars for you and the missus and the youngun," Dale said.

"That's a lot of money. I don't think we can afford it, Reed," Geneva said.

"If we are very careful the rest of the trip we might be able to," Reed looked at Geneva, surprised to see a veil of fear covering her eyes. They could be in Moncks Corner in two hours as opposed to two days of waiting plus another day of rough-riding in a stage.

"You two think about it awhile, and you too, Simon. Be a way we could make a little extra on this trip," Dale grinned. "Willard, I'll just have a heaping big bowl of stew. Want to save lots of room for doughnuts."

"I don't trust them," Geneva whispered to Reed.

"It's only two hours and it'll save two whole days. We can get a passenger train from there to wherever the line ends and be a lot closer to Lynchburg," Reed said.

"Train in Moncks Corner goes to Cheraw. It's about a day and a half with the stops and all," Willard told them after he'd served Simon and Dale.

"And from there to Lynchburg?" Reed asked.

"Train used to go that way but they've not got the tracks rebuilt yet after the war. Yanks tore them all up so we couldn't use 'em. From Cheraw, you'd go to High Point. That's about four days on the stage if you get all the right connections. At High Point you can get another passenger train right into Lynchburg. Should be about a two-day ride, maybe less," Willard told them. "That your final stoppin' place? Lynchburg?"

"Yes, it is," Geneva said.

"What're you goin' there for?" Simon asked from the other side of the room.

"To see my wife's aunt and look for a job," Reed said glibly.

"Good luck, mister," Dale laughed. "Jobs ain't layin' in the fence row no more. What're you lookin' for? Think you could learn to stoke a steam engine. The SC Railroad Company might hire you on."

"I'm a banker," Reed lied. "My wife was not happy in Savannah so I quit my job there. Surely there are banks in Lynchburg."

"Yep, but they ain't got much money since the war," Dale said. "You goin' to find that twenty dollars and ride up to Moncks Corner or not?"

"I think I will. Willard if you'd bring us two of

those big bowls of stew and some cornbread, the wife and I can eat before we leave. If I throw in an extra dollar would you see to it our trunks are loaded in the car?" he asked Dale.

"Sure will. Eat up and don't tarry though. Our schedule says we'll be leavin' in fifteen minutes," Dale grinned again. "And you will pay me before you get in that car."

"I'll pay you half when I get in that car," Reed said. "I'll give you the other half when my trunks are sitting in a hotel room in Moncks Corner."

Dale chuckled. "Fair enough."

"Willard, would you have any newspapers lying' around I could purchase?" Reed asked.

"Nope, ain't got a one. Don't have much call for them. Sometimes a passenger on the stage will leave one, but haven't even had that happen in a while now. Can tell you the biggest news around Pump Station, though. There's seven black men trying to buy six hun'urd and twenty acres of land right here in the area. A Bishop Richard Harvey Cain is the ringleader of the bunch of them. They're goin' to relocate right here and call the place Lincolnville, after President Lincoln, for freeing them. Whole bunch of them ought to read his speech he give that one time. Said he didn't think they ought to be owned, but he thought they all oughta be shipped back to Africa or wherever it was they come from. Namin' a whole town after the man who freed them but don't even want them to stay in the United States of America. Strikes me as a might odd," Willard said.

"Think they'll be able to buy the land?" Reed asked.

"No, they won't," Dale said. "Ain't no way they can come up with that much money."

"I wouldn't be surprised if they did," Simon said. "Be right odd to call Pump Pond something like Lincolnville, though. Maybe they'll change their minds."

"I doubt it," the stage driver and shotgun rider caught the conversation as they came through the door. "Heard tell they was right determined to own the land and make a town for their people. Going to build a church not far from right here. They got a notion that the railway will expand and more people will be coming up here. Willard, I'll have whatever you're servin' up. We got us a long night of drivin'. Got the horses changed out and the delivery loaded so, soon as we eat we'll be on our way."

"Railroad ain't never going to use Pump Pond for nothing but takin' on water and wood," Dale said. "People get these high falutin' ideas but it don't mean they'll 'come true."

Geneva ate her supper in silence. The stew was very good; the doughnuts, better. The last supper should at least taste good, she figured as she licked the sugar from her fingers, and then shuddered at such an idea. She'd shake off the feelings of doom. It was just that Pump Pond wasn't anything like a town. Just a stage and railway station all combined into one. Barely a wide spot in the road. Dark and dreary at that time of night, bringing on gloomy feelings down deep in her heart.

Geneva felt like she'd been locked in a jail when Dale slammed the door of the boxcar and bolted it shut. She wouldn't be a bit surprised if in two hours they were still rolling very fast right back to Savannah where the leering Dale would turn her over to the Savannah sheriff for a trumped up trial and speedy hanging.

"I know it's not comfortable but it's not any worse than the floor at the station. Want me to hold Angelina for a little while? You could lean on the trunk and maybe catch a nap. We'll be there in two hours and even though it will be late, we can check into a proper hotel," Reed said.

"We'll be dead in two hours," Geneva handed him the baby and the train began to move with a rumble. She grabbed the bars and held on tightly as everything began speeding past at breakneck speed. It was like riding a horse across the flatlands with the night air blowing across her face. At any other time, it would have been exhilarating, but right then Geneva was sure she was spending the last two hours of her life locked inside a moving jail.

Reed wished for a moment that he could go back and rethink his decision to give Dale the money for the fast trip. Unless his sense of direction was totally wrong they were going north but Dale's leering smile was disconcerting. "Geneva, I'm not real comfortable with those men, either, to tell you the truth, but if I didn't think I could protect you and Angelina, I wouldn't have taken the chance. Please trust me."

"Trust you. You don't know what you are asking Reed Hamilton. There's a part of me that will never trust any man again. You've been good to me and the baby but like you said, we're just traveling companions, thrown together by fate and kept there by the same. But trust you? That would mean more than I can give. Do your best to keep us safe and get us to Lynchburg and I'll be out of your life forever. Like you said when we bared our souls to each other, we'll never see each other again. Trust is something that builds, not something given away on a whim," she said.

"I will protect you," he said icily. He'd proven many times over since they'd been dumped on the side of the road in the South Carolina swamp land that he was a man of his word. He'd sworn he would take her safely to Lynchburg and he would, but blast it all to the devil's backyard, she could at least trust him. All relationships, whether they were simply friendships or something with more passion, were built on trust. And in the past three weeks, surely he'd done enough to earn her trust for the next two hours. It was a good thing that Hiriam Garner was already planted six feet down or Reed would have been very tempted to hang him all over again. And while he was at it, he just might string up Geneva's father at the same time. Neither of them deserved to have ever had someone so lovely in their lives. And they'd both shattered all and any trust of men for the rest of her life.

Geneva didn't bother to answer him. She sat down on the floor, propped her back against the trunk and imagined the countryside speeding past. The night air was sultry and sweat clung to her body like a tight fitting glove. It beaded up on her upper lip and rivulets ran down her neck, past the camisole and between her aching breasts. If Angelina didn't wake soon, she'd have to jostle her awake so she could nurse and take away the pain. She hoped Reed was right about being able to protect them. The baby whimpered and Reed handed her over to Geneva, who changed her wet clothing and fed her. Holding the baby tightly after she'd been lulled back to sleep by the moving train, Geneva settled into the corner made by the trunk against the wall of the train car and dozed.

Two hours was only a few seconds short of eternity. When the train rumbled to a halt every nerve in Reed's body was tingling. He hadn't slept a single second. As soon as the train was fully stopped he reached into his shoulder holster and removed his pistol, dropped it carefully to his side in the folds of his coat, sat down on his trunk and waited. His mother had a sixth sense about things and he trusted Geneva's feelings. Dale would bring some kind of trouble, he was sure.

"Ride okay?" Dale unbolted the door and slid it open. In the dim moonlight he was barely a silhouetted shadow.

"Just fine," Reed said.

His voice was tense, Geneva noticed as she came fully awake.

"Well, way I see it is you are now where you want to be and I can either hire a taxi to take you to the fanciest hotel in town and you can give me fifty dollars, or I can shoot all three of you and tell the boss man that you was bootleggin' a ride and drew on me. I got me a six-gun right here I'll throw down beside your cold dead bodies. Don't make me no never mind since I already got ten dollars. But a fancied up dude like you has got more. You ain't no banker. You're one of them gov'ment men. Don't know why you brought along the doxie but she ain't your wife, neither. Ain't even got on a gold ring and a fancied up man like you would have bought your woman a ring. So what'll it be? Money or a bullet?" He leveled a shotgun at Geneva.

"Money, I guess," Reed said.

Geneva's heart practically stopped beating.

"It's in my trunk. I'll have to open it to get it," Reed moved between Dale and Geneva.

"No, you ain't. Not without me bein' right beside you. You probably got a gun in there," Dale put a hand on the side of the car and hopped inside.

Before Dale could regain his balance and get complete control of the shotgun once more, Reed had crossed the car, kicked the gun from his hands and had his arm twisted up behind him in a painful position. "There's not a gun in my trunk. It's right in the middle of your shoulder blades. Now I think it's time for renegotiations, Dale."

The smaller man whined as Reed pranced him over to the side of the car and agilely pulled a length of lace from his pocket. Before Dale could suck in two lungfuls of air, he was tied securely to the bars. "Man, you can't leave me here. They'll fire me. I got a wife down in Ridgeland. Two boys to raise. Jobs ain't easy to come by."

"Should have thought of that before," Reed told him as he used the rest of the lace he'd removed from one of the petticoats in Geneva's trunks to tie his feet together.

"I'll get even. I saw in Ridgeland that the Savannah sheriff is lookin' for a big old tall woman just like your doxie over there. It might be her or it might not. But I'll tell that bounty hunter who's down there askin' questions that it is her and that you helped her kill her husband," Dale smarted off, trying to save face and dignity. To be found tied up with a lace from a woman's undergarments would bring a whole rainstorm of guffawing among the railroad men. Yes, sir, Reed Hamilton and that oversized cow of a woman would pay for this.

"You do what you have to do," Reed said. "Geneva, let's go."

She carried the baby and he dragged both trunks behind him across the rails to the station. It had already closed for the night but there was a livery stable with its lights still burning not far down the road, so that's where he set a course for.

"Why didn't you shoot the fool?" Geneva asked bluntly when she could find her voice again. "He'll make more trouble."

"I don't think so. He's all wind. He'll be the laughing stock of the whole railroad if he doesn't get himself untied by morning," Reed chuckled. "I sure wouldn't want to be found tied up with the lace off a woman's petticoat."

"You tore up one of my petticoats!" She stopped in the middle of the dusty street. "Which one? How did you get in my trunk?"

"I don't know which one it was. And you did nod off for a few minutes. I told you to trust me. I sure couldn't send out to the local general store for a rope could I?" he snapped at her.

"Hey, who's out there?" a man yelled from the doorway of the livery.

"Couple interested in renting a rig or hire a ride into town," Reed called back. The nerve of the woman to get angry when he'd just saved her life. Blasted petticoat would have been useless if she'd been lying back there dead.

"What're you doin' out at this time of night?" the man asked cautiously.

"We come in on the train from Pump Pond. We'd like to go to a hotel," Reed said.

"That'd be just a little ways. I got a rig ready. Was about to shut down the place and go on home myself. Had a late night. Horse died. I'll take you," the man said.

"Trusting, isn't he?" Geneva muttered.

"It's because he finally could see there was a woman with me. Man travels with a wife and baby in her arms don't usually plan on killing a livery stable owner for his rig and a dead horse," Reed said.

"What train'd you come in on?" the man asked after he'd snuffed the lights and brought the rig down to where Reed and Geneva waited.

"We're illegal," Reed smiled. "We got to Pump Pond and the stage manager told us it would be two days before we could get a stage north so we paid the train man to let us ride in an empty car."

"Dale's not supposed to do that. He's done been in trouble once for it. And there was that other time when they thought he might've been behind the killing of a wealthy man. Found him shot dead. Body thrown off the train not far from here," the man said. "He's goin' to get caught one of these days for sure and lose his job. Not that it would matter much. He's just a drifter. Ain't like he's got a family. He'd just find something else that wasn't really legal to do. You two are right lucky that you got out with your skins. That man is poison."

"I'm Reed Hamilton and this is my wife, Genny, and our daughter, Angelina," Reed said. "And my wife told me he wasn't to be trusted. Guess I should've listened to her."

"I'm Claud Smith, and women folks—they've got a sense about things like that. My wife is the same way. First few times she tried to tell me something about her 'feelings of doom' as I call them, I didn't listen. Didn't take me long to wise up, though. You been married twenty years like I been, you'll wizen up too, Mr. Hamilton. Well, here we are. This'd be the best hotel in town."

"What would I owe you?" Reed asked.

"Not a dime. It was right on my way home, anyway. Guess you'll be wantin' the next train north since you come from Pump Pond and that's south. It leaves at eight o'clock in the mornin'. Going to Cheraw, way up north or anywhere in between." He helped Reed get the two trunks into the lobby of the hotel where they awoke the desk clerk who'd been sleeping standing up, leaning on his elbows.

"And the one back toward Pump Pond, when does it leave?" Reed asked.

"They'll be loadin' it up with lumber and sendin' it back south by dawn the day after tomorrow. Why'd you ask?" Claud asked.

"Just asking," Reed smiled.

"Good luck to you both and listen to the little lady from here on in. It was only by the grace of God himself you two are walking around alive," Claud shook a finger at him.

"I told you so," Geneva whispered. Lord, but she'd be glad to get far enough away from Reed Hamilton that she never had to listen to him call her "the wife" or "the missus" again.

"And I suppose I'll have to hear that every day from here to Lynchburg," Reed said through tired gritted teeth.

"Maybe twice a day and six times if there's a

Sunday in between," she told him. "We need two rooms," she turned toward the desk clerk, who pushed the register book toward her. Without even thinking she signed, *Mr. and Mrs. Reed Hamilton,* with a flourish.

Chapter Eleven

Spanish moss hung from the trees like long bony fingers pointing at Geneva as she and Reed traveled from the hotel to the train station early that morning. Everywhere there was a riot of color. Red, pink, and white azaleas planted in every yard. Dripping sweet purple wisteria and the fragile magnolia blossoms opening up their enormous petals for a day of glory.

"Do you think that long arm of the sheriff could reach all the way here, Reed? I love this place. I could stay here with Angelina forever," she said.

"Don't know about the long arm of the sheriff. I would think you would be about a hundred and twenty five miles from Savannah. That's not near far enough for you to stop running. Besides they'll find Dale sometime today tied up with the petticoat lace and I wouldn't want to face his wrath," Reed chuckled.

Geneva sighed deeply.

"Don't worry, darlin', there're pretty flowers other places too. Why, your aunt might even have a whole garden for you and Angelina to enjoy," he told her.

"Don't call me darlin' and I'd as soon you not refer to me as the missus or the wife, either," she said.

"Whatever you say," Reed said mockingly. "Shall I refer to you as my doxie, then?"

"Oh, hush," Geneva said shortly. It had been a very short night and she'd slept little. She sure didn't have the energy to argue with Reed.

"We'll need to go to Cheraw," Reed told the ticket taker. "And I'd like a private car if it's available."

The man ran his finger down a list and nodded. "Got one from here to Cheraw. Family had it booked but had to go home early. Left a couple of days ago."

"Private car?" Geneva raised an eyebrow over widened blue eyes.

"The less people see you, the less chance that long arm we talked about will reach out to grab you. Besides, I like the privacy of my own car," he said.

"Leaving in about twenty minutes. Loading now. Johnny will come round and show you where to board and take your baggage. Arrival is about sunrise tomorrow morning. Names, please?" the man said as he counted the bills Reed laid on the counter and made change.

"Reed and Genny Hamilton and their daughter, Angelina," Reed said.

"You and the missus have a good trip," the man said. "And your meals will be served in the car today. Arrival is too early for breakfast in the morning though. I could order a midmorning snack if you've not had time for breakfast today."

"That would be very nice," Reed pushed the change back. "Thank you for your help. And could you send Johnny around with whatever newspapers you can gather up? I don't care how old or new they are."

"Yes, sir," the man smiled brightly. Wasn't every day a man gave him in excess of a five dollar tip.

Geneva gasped when Reed held her elbow and helped into the side door of a train car. In her wildest expectations she'd never thought to ride in something so elegant. Red silk covered the walls where brass sconces had already been lit, giving off a soft glow. Two huge four-poster beds, one on either end of the room, had bed coverings that matched the walls and a folding screen beside each with painted peacocks on the panels. Chairs so deep they reached out and beckoned to her to come and enjoy their comfort, were positioned to catch the light from the windows.

"Good grief, Reed, do you own a gold mine? I can never repay my half of something this grand," she whispered.

"I did not ask you to repay anything. And no, the Hamiltons no longer own gold mines. Daddy had a couple back before the war began but he'd already sold them off when he died," Reed said.

"Who are you?" Geneva sank down into one of the chairs, wallowing in the way it embraced her.

"I'm Harry Reed Hamilton of the Love's Valley Hamiltons in Pennsylvania," he took the other chair and for just a moment shut his eyes to enjoy the comfort of it.

"I know that, but how can you afford this? Did you rob a bank or something?" she asked.

Johnny rapped on the door and poked his head in without being invited before Reed could answer. "Your trunks are here. I'll get them inside and then the train will be leaving in five minutes. I've told the dining room to bring you a midmornin' snack at ten. Dinner is at straight up noon and supper at six. If you want something in between tell the steward. Or if you want a late-night snack, just tell him. Oh, and here's as many newspapers as I could find." He handed Reed a stack of papers and loaded the trunks, then was gone just moments before the train whistle blew and the car began to move.

"Want to lay Angelina on one of the beds and read awhile?" Reed asked.

"Yes, I do," Geneva answered. "But Reed, what if she wets on that fine bed?"

He chuckled. "Then that one belongs to you tonight. I intend to sleep soundly in a dry bed. Try folding up several of her blankets and put them under her. That might work." He was already rifling through the papers to see which one was the most current.

Geneva did what he suggested, laid the baby on the bed, and watched her for a few minutes. Poor little thing had been shifted from pillar to lamppost ever since the morning she was born. She should have had a cradle all of her own to lie in when she wasn't being fed or diapered, but instead she'd had to make do with a sling. And all the bustling in stagecoaches—it was a wonder she wasn't sick from all of it. But she seemed to have a constitution of steel even though she had been about three weeks early.

Angelina stretched to her full length of barely more than twenty inches and snuggled right down in the soft bed. She didn't shut her eyes in sleep but watched the sunlight dance through the windows of the car. Geneva smiled at her daughter. She'd be all right, that one would. She might even be the first woman to step up to the polls and cast her vote for President of the United States. At least that's the way Geneva intended to raise her. Independent. Strong.

"Hey, there's a man up in Ohio by the name of Lucian B. Smith who has patented something called barbed wire," Reed said aloud. "It's a twisted wire with pieces that poke out to string between the fence posts. Says here it will revolutionize the way we build fences and speculates that it won't be long until free range is closed and all ranchers will fence in their property."

"I hate so much change," Geneva picked up a paper from the table in front of the two chairs and glanced through the headlines. "Why couldn't things have stayed the way they were? Change brings so many heartaches."

"Yes, but it also brings progress," Reed said.

"Oh, my," Geneva gasped. "President Johnson is telling the world that the United States has bought Alaska. Three hundred seventy five million acres for more than seven million dollars. Where is Alaska, Reed? And in this war-torn country, where in the world did they find that much money? That's got to be all the money in the whole world," she said.

"Not quite. Actually, it's a very wise decision and money well spent. Who knows what's up there under all that cold. Could be something we'll be right glad we own in the future. Alaska is an almighty big chunk of land way up north. I plan to go there someday now that the country owns it. I might find a business venture there to sink some Hamilton dollars into," he said.

"Hamilton dollars? You never did answer me, Reed. Did you rob a bank?" Her blue eyes narrowed as she stared at the man she thought she'd begun to know.

"No, I don't recollect any Hamiltons robbing banks. We came over here from England way back when. My great-grandfathers made some very wise investments and my grandfathers stepped right up when it was their turn and made even more. My father did the same and now the three of us Hamilton boys and my sister, Indigo, have our fingers in lots of pies. We had gold mines and sold them. We've got interest in some shipping ventures, some cattle ranches, some horses," he said as he scanned over the inside of the paper.

Geneva stared at him unabashedly. "Are you telling me you are rich?"

"Rich is in the eye of the beholder," he chuckled. "I don't think we'd have quite enough to buy Alaska from President Johnson, but then I never did have a hankering to have to take care of three hundred seventy five million acres. So does that change your mind, the knowledge that I'm not poor, about pretending to be my wife?"

"I wouldn't care if you owned Alaska and the whole rest of the United States with England and France thrown in for good measure. I'm not going to ever marry again and pretending to be a wife is almost as bad as that. Money can't buy happiness and it brings on more grief than I ever want to face again," she said.

"I'm not Hiriam," Reed clenched his teeth. "Don't judge all men by one rotten apple, Geneva. There are lots of good men out there who'd be glad to have someone as lovely as you to call his wife."

"Thank you for that. Now let's drop the subject. Oh, my goodness," she exclaimed holding up the front page of the second paper she picked up. "Look here. Over in England the British parliament has rejected a law on women's suffrage. I didn't even know things had got far enough for women to be considered anything but servants. Well, they might have tossed it out this time, but the time is coming."

"You're all ready for that change, huh?" Reed asked, liking the way the red walls and the bright sunshine pouring in from the window gave a glow to Geneva's cheeks.

"Like you said, it brings progress," she mumbled and kept reading.

"Says here that an outlaw name of Jesse James robbed a bank in Richmond, Virginia, and got away with four thousand dollars," Reed was glad to have someone to converse with and wondered if this was what his parents had shared before his father died. They often sat in the parlor, newspapers scattered among them, talking. That memory hadn't surfaced in Reed's mind in a very long time. He smiled.

"Is that funny?" Geneva asked.

"No, I was enjoying a vision from the past," Reed said.

"Of robbing banks?" Geneva laid her paper aside and raised an eyebrow.

"No, of my parents reading the papers together late in the evening. My brothers and I would have our chores done so we'd be free to saddle up our horses and ride the length of the valley or do whatever we pleased. I remembered more than once coming in and hearing them discuss whatever was in the papers," he said.

"Tell me about your valley," she crossed her legs primly at the ankles and folded her hands in her lap. Her traveling dress was in bad need of a good washing and not just a brushing and suddenly looked dowdy in the rich surroundings.

"Love's Valley is a narrow valley between the Blacklog and Shade mountains. Seven miles long and between a quarter and a half-mile wide. Three and a half miles from a town named Orbisonia and a little more than two miles into Shirleysburg which is where we do most of our business. If we can't get what we need in Shirleysburg we can go six miles into Mt. Union. There's a shale pit on the ridge on the way down to Shirleysburg. It's not a big place, built a hundred years ago by George Croghan. There's the Shirleysburg Female Seminary there and the Shirleysburg Foundry, which is part of the Pennsylvania Iron Furnaces. It's got its own newspaper, *The Shirleysburg Herald.* And a general store that keeps a good stock for the ladies to shop from as well as about anything else anyone would need, and there's a tailor, a hotel. . . . Just a small town. But the valley, that's home. My brothers are back there and my sister, along with my mother."

"Does it snow in your world?" She asked.

"Knee-deep to a tall man or a tall woman," he smiled and his eyes sparkled. "Have you ever been in snow country?"

"I've seen it snow but never enough to play in or build a snowman or make ice cream out of it. There were a few tinkers who got stuck up in the north in the snow season. They'd tell us stories. It sounded so grand," she said wistfully.

"It's wonderful, especially if there's not a war going on. We have all four seasons. In winter the snow and cold takes your breath away. But we work hard during the other seasons and other than routine chores we can stay out of the bitter cold. In spring everything turns minty green and the spirit soars at being able to get outside and work again. Then summer comes and there are picnics and socials. Then fall and harvest-ing . . ." he said.

"You're a poet, Reed Hamilton. A homesick poet," she laughed.

The sound of her feminine giggle echoed in the car like the tapping of fine silver against a cut crystal glass. It was the first time he'd seen her really smile; the first time he'd heard her laugh. It was as musical as angels playing harps on the steps leading up to an open door to heaven.

"Not me. Now Rueben, he might be a poet—he's the middle son. Quiet. He's the one who thought everything through and never took chances. At least not until he got tangled up with Adelida. I guess there were some chances there, all right," Reed said.

Geneva still smiled, her blue eyes twinkling. She might never see this man again but he was entertaining her with his family stories and she wanted more. For just one day she would be a rich lady traveling with her husband and listening to tales of a foreign land called Pennsylvania where there was a long, snaky valley called of all things, Love's Valley. She wondered who on earth would name a piece of ground such a thing.

"Chances? Rueben took chances?" she cocked her head to one side.

"Oh, yes, not that he wanted to," Reed chuckled, amazed that something as lighthearted as a laugh could come from his chest after all he'd been forced to endure these past weeks. "You see, he was sent to Louisiana at the same time I went to Georgia. My older brother Monroe went to Texas. We all left Love's Valley together that morning. Indigo stood on the porch pitching a fit about all her brothers finally coming home and now the government was stealing them again. Ellie, that's our cousin who lives in Love's Valley, since her parents were killed by Rebels in the fire that took most of Chambersburg, tried to shush her. I remember Ellie told us each how proud she was that we'd all survived the war and that the next months would go by fast. Indigo pouted but we rode up the lane, all three of us abreast on our horses. When Monroe was on his way home from Texas, he literally ran across a woman sitting on a trunk in the middle of the road. Her name is Douglass and she'd run away with a man from Philadelphia. She thought they'd be married but he had other ideas which weren't honorable, so she left him. Monroe, being a gentleman, couldn't leave her on the side of the road so he offered to escort her to the next town."

Geneva leaned forward. "Did he fall in love with this Texan?"

"Oh, yes, but not before she'd led him on one hellacious merry chase from north Texas all the way to Love's Valley. When they reached the valley, her brothers, who'd been sent to fetch her home, finally caught up with her, and according to Ellie there was quite the melee that evening. Ellie scratching one of the brothers on the face and a real fisticuffs fight," Reed said. "The letter made me laugh until I held my sides. Douglass and Monroe were both miserable with the whole thing and finally Monroe stepped up and admitted he'd fallen in love with her and they were married the next week right there at the farmhouse."

"Ah," Geneva sighed wishing he'd go on or at least give her more details. She wondered if he had the letters from his cousin describing the whole wedding.

What had the dress looked like and were the azaleas blooming. Did she wear roses in her hair.

"But that's Monroe's story. Then there's Ellie's," Reed said.

A rapping on the end door brought them out of the fairy tale land of love and to their senses. They both jumped as if they'd been indulging in a kiss rather than just enjoying each other's company that morning. Reed answered the door to find a steward with their morning tea.

"Where shall I set up?" he asked.

"Right between the two chairs would be fine," Reed motioned to where Geneva had buried her face in another newspaper. He wondered if he'd bored her with the tales of his family. Perhaps she was only listening because she felt like she should be polite since he'd paid for a private railcar.

The man and a helper set up a small table, laid it out with a silver coffee pot filled with steaming, black liquid but not as black as Reed usually drank, Geneva noticed. A bowl of fresh fruit; apples, bananas, oranges and sliced cantaloupe. A tray of small sandwiches that looked like they'd have chicken in them and another tray of cookies and small pastries. There was enough food on the table to last them all day. She couldn't imagine what they'd bring for dinner and supper if this was only a snack.

"Thank you so much," Reed slipped the man a tip as he went out the door.

"Ah, food," he picked up a sandwich and bit off a healthy chunk.

"Can you tell me about Ellie while we eat?" she asked, filling a small plate with all kinds of delicacies. She wondered if her mother had lived like this before she eloped with Daniel O'Grady. Had she given up a life of absolute luxury to live in a tinker's wagon and travel all over the south fixing pots and pans?

Reed grinned. "I don't want to bore you."

"Bore me. It's fascinating," she said.

And he believed her.

"Well, Ellie is the one who writes the most detailed letters so when she and Colum got back from their adventure, I got several long, long letters. Colum is one of the brothers who came to rescue Douglass from her fiancé you see. On the night of the big wedding between Douglass and Monroe, Ellie found that her fiancé was only marrying her for her money. So Douglass talked Ellie into calling it off. Ellie wrote me that Douglass offered to shoot the scoundrel and bury him under the compost pile but Ellie declined. I suppose for a while there though she wished she would have taken Douglass up on the offer," Reed ate several cookies and drank half a cup of coffee.

To Geneva it was an eternity before he started to talk again.

"The man hit Ellie so hard one day that he knocked her out, then kidnapped her and took her away to the backside of Blacklog Valley where one of his evil cohorts had a trapper's cabin. Chained her to the wall and left her to die because she wouldn't marry him," Reed said.

Cold chills chased up and down Geneva's spine. "What happened?" she whispered.

"Well, Douglass wasn't believing a bit of the fellow's story about how Ellie hated having a Rebel in the house so bad she ran off and was pushing for a speedy marriage so she wouldn't have to abide under the same roof as Douglass. So she sent her brother, Colum, who was one of the best trackers in the Confederate army to find her. He's the one who found her with a raging fever and right next door to death, chained in that cabin. Took him a week or more to bring her back to life enough to walk out of that forsaken place and back to Shirleysburg. He wasn't a happy man that he'd gotten snowed in and had to winter in Pennsylvania but Douglass was very glad to have him. When spring thaw came, he was on his way back to Texas when this fellow that had treated Ellie so badly and his cohorts decided to rob the bank. Ellie walked in on it and Colum thought they'd killed her. Monroe wrote that Colum came out of the bank carrying Ellie, who was all bloody. Said he was about crazy with grief. Turned out though that the outlaws had killed one another trying to shoot her and it was their blood on Ellie. Colum proposed to her right there on the main street of Shirleysburg in a loud voice because Ellie's hearing was off. The bullets, you know, so close to her ears had caused her to be deaf for a little while. Anyway, they wound up getting married and now they're building a house in Love's Valley too. It might even be finished by the time I get home.

Douglass and Monroe's house is done and they're expecting a baby this summer. It might already be born too. Last letter I had was from Indigo and said the baby wasn't there yet but that Douglass was big as a barn."

He loaded up his plate and began to eat again. The sandwiches were tasty enough for railroad food. His mother made better chicken salad though. The cookies were fairly good. Indigo's cinnamon snaps would beat them all to the devil but it was all much better than that basket of bread and cheese he and Geneva survived on the first day they boarded the stage outside of Ridgeland. That seemed like months and months ago rather than only days. Back when she wasn't ever going to travel under the pretense of being his wife, before she could brazenly pick up a quill pen and sign herself into a hotel as Mrs. Reed Hamilton.

Friends, that's what they'd become through the trials of traveling together. He'd never had a female friend before. Lots of acquaintances. Lots of ladies he'd flirted with and escorted to one function or another. But a friend? No, he couldn't say he had had a friend of the feminine gender. It was a revelation; one he'd have to ponder on for a while.

"You didn't tell me about Rueben, yet, and how is it that all three of you left at the same time but Monroe got home last year and you're just now going?" She finished the food and set the plate aside, checked Angelina who was sleeping soundly and went back to the chair. She wondered briefly how much a chair like this one cost. Would her Aunt Minnie have such fine things in her house?

"Monroe was in Texas. Rueben in Louisiana," Reed's eyes were heavy.

"Don't you go to sleep before you tell me about Rueben," Geneva shook her finger at him.

"Rueben, ah, now there is a story. But why don't we take a nap and then hear that one?" Reed teased.

"I couldn't sleep until I hear about him. He's the quiet one you said. Yet, he took home a Southern bride too. Tell me and then we'll take a long, lazy nap," she said.

"If a nap on a real bed is my prize for being the storyteller, then you shall hear about Rueben," Reed's brown eyes twinkled more than Geneva had ever seen.

"Rueben is the middle child. The quiet one who sat back and studied a situation before he jumped in the middle of it. Totally unlike Monroe or me. He'd finished his time in Louisiana. The last thing he needed to do was go to the bank and take care of his business there when he quite literally ran into Adelida who was also going into the bank. Her sister had been killed in a freakish accident the night before and her brother-in-law had told her she'd better be out of town before the next day's end or he'd kill her. She had reason to believe the bullet that killed her sister might have been intended for her anyway since her brother-in-law hated her," Reed sipped his lukewarm tea.

Geneva waited patiently. So other people had suffered hardships too. Sometimes when the wolf named difficulty was scratching at a person's door, they tended to think they were the only ones in the world about to be eaten alive.

"Anyway, they collided in front of the bank and Adelida went tumbling, petticoats flying and Rueben landing smack on top of her. I'd have loved to have seen old stable Rueben's face," Reed laughed so hard he had to draw his handkerchief from his pocket to dry his eyes.

Geneva giggled at Reed more than the story. The last time she'd seen a man laugh so openly and loudly was back when Sylvie was dating her husband-to-be. He'd played a trick on her and laughed just like Rueben was doing. Like friends. She and Reed had become friends who could share good times as well as troubled ones. However, she did feel sorry for Adelida. Poor, poor woman, to be in that position right in public.

"So he helps her up, introduces himself, and they go into the bank together after he's apologized a hundred times. Turns out there were robbers in the bank and they thought since Rueben and Adelida had come in together they were man and wife. Kind of like the old black woman thinking we were married because we were sitting in the road together," he said.

High color filled her cheeks. The other Hamilton men might have had adventures that led to marriage, but Reed would not, and the difference lay both in Geneva and the baby sleeping on the bed. Douglass and Adelida and even Ellie hadn't been married; they weren't wanted by the law; and they didn't have a new baby. But all that was moot because of the fact that Geneva didn't want a husband. Not ever.

"Go on," she finished her tea and set the china cup aside.

"Rueben, big and stable as he is, thought he could prevent the robbery. Never knew him to be a hero type. Must have been the fall outside that still had his brains addled. Anyway, he went to draw his gun, and one of the robbers gave him a good hit on the head. Sent him sprawling and when he opened his eyes, he was lying in Adelida's lap. Everyone in the place thought they were a married couple, you've got to remember. So he looks up at her and not only didn't know her but didn't know who he was either. The doctor who sewed him up treated Adelida as his wife. And she saw a way out of New Orleans by just letting everyone keep right on thinking that."

"Oh, my, she said she was married to him and she wasn't," Geneva gasped.

"Yes, took a big chance and did just that. They boarded the ship where he had reservations and she told him that the doctor had said they were to have separate beds until he remembered everything." Heat filled Reed's face making it blood red. Men folks didn't tell ladies things like that. Not even if they had delivered their baby for them or if they'd lived in close quarters for weeks. And Geneva was a lady, no matter what her background was or what she'd been through.

"And?" Geneva waited, wondering why the loquacious Reed had suddenly stammered and stopped.

"And he didn't remember until they were stranded by a big ocean storm on a small island. No one there but the two of them so they had lots of time and opportunity to get the fight out of the way," Reed grinned. "They stopped and visited me in Savannah a couple of months ago, then wound up getting married when they got to Love's Valley. But I forgot, they found a fortune in pirate's treasure on that island, where Hamilton Enterprises recovered them, and Adelida is a rich woman now in her own rights. Now can we take a nap?" he asked.

"Yes, but while we are going to Lynchburg, I want more details. To think you've had these stories hidden in your memories and have sat there like a bump on a log all these days when you could have entertained me," she said.

He sat the screen up between them and peeled off his coat and shirt, along with his shoes and socks and stretched out on the most comfortable bed he'd had in weeks.

Geneva loosened the jacket of her traveling suit, diapered and fed Angelina, and wished she could take the railroad car all the way to Lynchburg.

Neither of them slept.

Chapter Twelve

Geneva wore the light blue dress, trimmed in ecru colored lace with a fashionable hat to match. She looked the part of a lady traveling with her wealthy husband and new baby, but inside she was still the too-tall woman who'd been used as collateral in a card game. She sat in the lawyer's office, Angelina in her lap, Reed beside her, waiting for the man to look over a sheaf of papers. The brass plate on the door and the fancy engraving on the glass window said he was Jonathan Lawrence and with his portly manner, gold watch fob and balding head, he looked like a Jonathan. Geneva squinted slightly and tried to imagine him a young man being called Johnny but it didn't work. He was much too staid. Perhaps he'd been born full-grown and had skipped childhood, going straight from the birthing room to the lawyer's office.

"Your Aunt Minnie was quite a woman," he said in a meek little voice, sounding like it came from a twelve-year-old boy whose voice hadn't changed yet.

So something of him hadn't snuck completely past the childhood days, Geneva thought as she nodded and waited.

"Did you ever meet her?" he asked.

"No, my mother eloped with my father, Daniel O'Grady and the family disowned her for it. By the time I was big enough to ask questions, it was all ancient history," she said. "I was just hoping she was still living so I could get to know her."

"Your grandparents, Viola and Pete Edmonds, were very disappointed when their lovely daughter eloped with that tinker. So was I since I'd offered for her hand," Mr. Lawrence said. "Your mother was the most beautiful creature to ever come out of Lynchburg, Virginia. Spirited too."

"I'd like to know more about her as a young woman than you could tell me this morning," Geneva looked the man straight in the eye without blinking and wondered what kind of girl she'd be if he'd been her father.

"You look exactly like her except for the height. She was a tall woman but not nearly as tall as you are. But then you'd know that. How old were you when she died?"

"Fifteen," Geneva answered.

"Yes, my dear, we will have to have tea some afternoon and let me tell you more about your mother and that side of your family. Minnie was the older, plain daughter. A bit touched, some said. But she ran that plantation like a man after your grandfather and grandmother died. Did a fine job of it too. Was a shame it came to an end by Sherman's hand. I think that's what killed her in the end, knowing that all those years had literally gone up in smoke. She sold the land and gave the money to a college for women. All but what it took to buy a little house in town here and keep her going the last year of her life. She told me there wasn't room for her in the new world. Last year she died. House is still standing over there a block off Main Street. You'd be welcome to stay there while Mr. Hamilton goes on to Washington for his business. But it's already been sold and the new owners will take possession in two weeks. They bought it lock, stock and barrel. However," he leaned forward and whispered, "if there would be a few small keepsake family items you'd like to take for yourself, I'm sure that would be fine. The money from the sale has been donated to the same college for women."

"I see," Geneva's heart fell to the floor. She had the money she'd taken from the jar in the cellar but that wouldn't last out a month if she had to pay room and board. She wasn't trained to do any kind of work other than being a tinker and besides who'd look after Angelina?

"She left a box, though. Gave it to me a month before she died and said if her sister, Eva, ever came back I was to give it to her. So I suppose you being the legal heir to Eva should have it. There's letters in there from Eva to her, written through the years. I suppose Minnie never did hold with the same opinion her parents did of Eva's chosen life. And there's some stock in a New York company that had to do with coal and navigation. I could look into it for you, but my advice would be since you have no ties here, that you and your husband travel on to Pennsylvania and then look into it from there. It seems legal enough. Your grandfather bought into it back in the twenties. There are a few letters of correspondence between him and some fellow named LeHigh about the company. Seems it brings coal out up there and ships it to Philadelphia," he said.

"Thank you," Geneva said when Mr. Lawrence set a wooden box on the desk top.

"Sorry I couldn't be the bearer of better news," he said.

"We are grateful to you for keeping these things for her and for allowing us to stay in the house," Reed said. "I'll be gone to Washington for three days. Geneva will enjoy having those days to rest and recuperate from this long journey. However, one afternoon, I'm sure she would be glad to have you stop by for tea," Reed shook the man's hand and picked up the box, amazed at how light it was. Lifetimes reduced to what paper could be packed in a box he could fit under his arm. Somehow it didn't seem right.

Clouds hung low in the sky, promising rain, bringing humidity so thick it smothered Geneva and Reed as they got out of the taxi in front of a small town-house. Painted white with azaleas blooming profuse-ly in the front yard and a swing on the porch that wrapped itself around one corner, it beckoned to Geneva like a mother calling her child home to sup-per. It was the reality of a dream she'd had since she was a child, to live in a white house with a swing and flowers. A dream she'd never shared because it was too far-fetched to ever come true. A dream that was real now, only for a few days and then would be jerked out from under her. She should have stayed with Liam and gone back to the tinkers. Sylvie would have taken her and Angelina in. *But then what?* she asked herself as Reed slipped the skeleton key into the lock and swung open the door.

"Nice little place," Reed took it all in as Geneva stood in the middle of the foyer floor, almost stupefied in her weariness. Was this the day she would crack under all the pressure she'd endured the past weeks? He hoped not. Tomorrow he would travel by train to Washington D. C. He'd already sent a telegram to President Johnson, asking to schedule a brief meeting. The third day, he'd come back and hopefully Geneva would have made up her mind about where she want-ed to go. Basically, he'd done what he'd promised and had fulfilled his vow to see her safely to Lynchburg. Now he could finish the last leg of his journey home to Love's Valley much faster without a woman and baby to hold him back.

The taxi driver carried their trunks up the stairs to

the two small bedrooms at the top of the landing and set them beside the doors. He was gone five full minutes before either Reed or Geneva spoke. She stared at the family painting hanging above the mantel in the sitting room. Her mother, looking much as Geneva did right then, in a portrait with her own mother and father and sister. Minnie really had been the plain sister, just missing Eva's beauty by a nose that was slightly too narrow and too long, lips that were just a touch too firm, eyes set too close together. She looked like the feminine version of her father, while Eva had inherited all her mother's lovely qualities. Angelina's whimpers finally brought Geneva out of the past and into the present.

"There are two bedrooms up here," Reed said from the top of the stairs. "One looks like your Aunt Minnie occupied it. Has a lot of her personal touches. You can have it. The other one is evidently the guest room. Doesn't look like anyone ever stayed here."

"That's fine. I'll see if there's any food in the kitchen and make us dinner after I feed Angelina. You might open the windows up there and then a couple down here and see if we can get a breeze going. It's hot enough to fry a body's brains," she sat down in a rocking chair close to the fireplace. In the eerie silence of the closed house she could feel the past and the present combining. If only she was clairvoyant enough to see the future in that moment it would bring her comfort, but she couldn't and she had absolutely no idea what she was going to do.

"I would guess there is nothing in the kitchen to

eat," Reed took the armchair on the far side of the room after he'd opened the windows. "I'll go to the grocer and buy enough food to keep you while I'm gone to Washington. It's too hot to fire up the cook-stove for dinner. I'll buy a loaf of bread and some cheese. Maybe some fresh fruit if it's available."

She nodded. She already owed him more than she'd ever be able to repay. In three days, she'd tell him good-bye and they'd part company. Then she might be lucky to even have a loaf of bread and cheese for her meals. Fancy railroad cars with their snacks of sandwiches and tea would only be a memory. Even hotel food would be something she barely remembered. Fresh fruit would be a luxury she sure wouldn't be able to afford unless she picked it herself from a tree in the wilds. Perhaps the thing she should do would be to buy a wagon, outfit it with tinker supplies, and go back on the road. It was the one life she understood. For the last six years of her father's life he'd been drunk ninety percent of the time and she'd learned the art of fixing pots and pans and even knew how to work on farm equipment. No one seemed to mind a woman doing the work, especially one who was bigger than they were.

"So anything in particular you want for the next three days?" he asked on his way out the door.

"Anything will be fine," she said. "Don't overbuy. It'll just be me."

He whistled as he walked down the street toward the main part of town. But then he could whistle, she reasoned with herself as she buttoned up the front of her pretty dress. After all, he'd been a true gentleman the whole trip and he'd delivered what he'd promised that day the wild hog had almost eaten her daughter. She looked down into the sleeping face of her baby. Angelina, who'd begun to fill out the wrinkles in her skin and look even more like Eva with her delicate nose and rosebud mouth. Looking up at the baby's grandmother, Geneva could see exactly what her daughter would look like in twenty years. Hopefully, she'd stop growing before she reached six feet though.

She carried the baby upstairs to the room where Reed had put her things. A four-poster bed covered in a handmade quilt of many bright colors didn't begin to fill the room. She'd expected a tiny bedroom from the looks of the front of the house and the living room. Evidently the structure was narrow in the front and much deeper in length. A dresser with a mirror held all kinds of feminine things. A silver hairbrush, tarnished with age and lack of use. A matching mirror with pits in the glass. Empty perfume bottles with only the scent of what had been inside still lingering. A picture of a young man, eyes wide open as he waited for the camera to do its work. Geneva picked it up and wondered if it was someone Minnie had loved who'd forsaken her or had died before their love could be acknowledged.

"Angelina, here is our history," she murmured. "Our history, which we have three days to uncover and then we have to decide about our future."

The box the lawyer had given them was set on a

chair, a nice big overstuffed one like the one she'd fall-en in love with on the railway car from Moncks Corner to Cheraw. Could that have only been five days before? It seemed a lifetime ago. A time when she had finally realized Reed Hamilton was her friend. She'd prodded him for more stories about his family as they rode stagecoach after coach. Now she wished she hadn't. If would have been much easier to wave good-bye to him one final time if she didn't know him so well.

She set the box on the table in front of the chair. Her aunt had sat in this chair during the past year every evening and read or did stitching. She'd lived, most likely loved that boy in the picture, and died, and Geneva had only known her as a name. Not a real per-son with a kind voice, or a sharp tongue, or who could make good cornbread or whose cookies always burned on the bottom side.

She opened the box. On one side tied in a bundle were the papers the lawyer had mentioned about a coal and navigation company. With her luck the com-pany probably had long gone defunct, or the war had changed the whole thing. She didn't even untie them. She'd have Reed look at them when he came home from Washington.

"Now where did that notion come from?" she mut-tered. "Reed won't be coming home anymore than I'm really at home. He'll be coming back here and that will be that. I guess the only way I'll know what the coal business is worth is to go to New York and find out. Is that what I'm supposed to do, Angelina?" she asked the baby on the bed. "I'll think on it until he comes back. Maybe if I gave him the money I have he would consent to let me travel with him as far as Love's Valley and I could buy passage on to New York to see if we do indeed have money or if we're destitute."

She picked up the small bundle of letters and untied the faded pink satin ribbon. Did she really want to open the letters? She'd known her mother as a loving, kind person, always ready to give to anyone who needed it, whether it was a helping hand, something from the wagon, or sweet words to Daniel to keep him out of the liquor.

She fingered them. Counted them. Ten letters in all addressed to Minerva Edmonds. She opened the first one, dated the month after Geneva was born:

Dearest Sister,

I'm so so sorry for running away without telling you good-bye and without any explanation. I couldn't marry Jonathan Lawrence. Daddy said I would or else since there was that trouble with Davie. Daniel reminds me of Davie, Minnie. He's free-spirited and funny and he makes me laugh. But I fear, a year down the road now, that I made the wrong decision to turn my back on all I knew. It's too late now to go back and I'll make the best of the bed I've made. I'll sleep in it and not complain for it was my own impulsive decision that put me here. I have a new baby daughter, Geneva, who looks exactly like me and Momma. If I have anoth-

er daughter I intend to name her Minnie after you,
but this one Daniel insisted on naming Geneva.
She's holding my heart in her little hands, Minnie,
even though she's only a few weeks old. I would
give anything to bring her home and let you hold
her. I know you can't answer my letters since you
wouldn't know where to send them, but it helps me
to write them so occasionally I'll send one to you.
Please know that I love you. I love Momma and
Poppa, too, but I couldn't be shackled forever in a
marriage of their choosing.
                                    Your Eva, who misses you

An hour later Reed returned from the general store
in a taxi coach with several packages. He and the driver unloaded them in the living room and he tiptoed
up the stairs to find Geneva sitting in a chair, letters
strewn all around her, tears streaming down her face.

"Geneva, what has happened?" he was amazed. In
all the hardship of the journey, the birthing of a child,
the knowledge her father was dead, killing the man in
the riot, her husband hung before her very eyes, she
hadn't cried like that.

"Nothing. I just got to know my mother a lot better
this afternoon. And I'm coming to realize the importance of being totally honest and standing up for
myself," she said, carefully stuffing the letters back
into their faded envelopes.

The first drops of rain peppered against the windows as the two of them went down the stairs. The

kitchen was through a doorway behind the parlor and in a silent joint effort the two of them prepared a simple lunch of bread, cheese, and apples. Geneva insisted that Reed build a small fire in the cookstove so they could make coffee and tea.

"The rain is already cooling things off," she motioned toward the raised window where the pretty embroidered curtains fanned in with the soft breeze. "And probably getting the curtains wet too, but it smells so nice I'm not going to shut the window."

"So you like the smell of summer rain?" Reed asked.

"I do. I love it," she said. "Reed, I just read in those letters . . ." she swallowed hard but the lump in her throat refused to go down, "I just read that my mother made a big mistake when she ran off with my father. She longed to come back home. Missed her family. Missed her sister. But she couldn't."

"I'm sorry," he reached across the table and patted her hand.

She was amazed at the feelings his touch evoked. Something soft and mushy settled into her stomach and a shock chased down her spine. A longing that she couldn't identify, had never felt before. Most likely, she surmised, it was nothing more than hunger combined with the shedding of a whole river of tears.

Reed pulled his hand away reluctantly. Touching her hand, so soft and warm, had caused his heart to race. That was an emotion he was supposed to experience with a woman from Love's Valley, not a tinker's daughter in southern Virginia. It wasn't accurate; he reasoned with his heart it was just the byproduct of a man who'd been cooped up with the woman too long and who'd just witnessed her tears.

He'd be very careful not to touch her again. Not even to take her elbow to escort her. Tomorrow he'd be on his way to Washington. After that the only thing in his future was Love's Valley.

Chapter Thirteen

Soothing rain continued to fall all through the night, cooling the temperatures somewhat. Good sleeping weather, Reed had said after they'd eaten supper and were sitting before the cold fireplace. He slept well, awakening when the sun should have been brightening the day, but a fine mist still fell and the sky promised a gray day. At least, he thought as he packed a valise, it would be a little cooler for Geneva and Angelina while he was gone. Then a pang stabbed him in the heart. He already started missing both of them and he wasn't even gone yet. He tried reasoning with himself. Sure, he'd miss them. It was natural. They'd all three spent every waking minute together for several weeks. He and Geneva had become friends. He'd be foolish to think he could walk out the front door of the house and into the misty morning and not miss what had been attached to him for that long and with such intensity. But the trip would do him good. It would be the first break to create a cushion for the final good-byes.

Geneva had stoked up a fire in the cookstove when he reached the kitchen. Her thick blond hair hung down her back in a single braid. She wore the old dress she'd had on when he first met her, girded in around the waist with a belt. One of her Aunt Minnie's snowy white bibbed aprons made her look as if she truly was the mistress of the house, preparing breakfast for her husband. The flush on her cheeks from the stove's heat gave color to her cheeks. The freckles popped up across her nose and a wisp of hair had glued itself to the moisture on her forehead. Reed thought she was breathtakingly beautiful.

"Something smells good," he said.

"Just hoe cakes. I'd've made pancakes but there're no eggs. There is lots of homemade jelly, though, so you can at least leave on a full stomach. If you're booking a private car, I expect they'll bring you whatever you want," she said, expertly flipping the dough over to brown the other side.

"I didn't get a car. The trip is only a day long. I'll be there before bedtime tonight. The taxi will be here in a few minutes, but I've got time to eat, and thank you fixing it for me," he pulled up a chair and pried the wax out of the top of a jar of what looked to be plum jelly.

"And you'll be back late in the evening, on the day after tomorrow?" she asked.

"Yes, that's right. Maybe you could ask the lawyer to tea tomorrow to help pass the day," he said.

"Maybe so," she said.

An awkward silence filled the room as he spread jelly on the hoe cakes and ate his fill. Reed hated good-byes. Absolutely hated them. He'd detested telling his mother and sister good-bye when he left for the war. Perhaps the sensible thing for him to do was to keep going and not even look back when he waved from the taxi. It would be easier than coming back and having to tell Geneva good-bye a second time. He didn't even want to think about never seeing Angelina again. A knot formed in his chest, one that ached and ached. Geneva would probably stay in Lynchburg or else ride the train to New York to see if the stock she'd been left in that coal company was worth anything. And he'd go on home to Love's Valley, which suddenly didn't look as bright and shiny as it had a few weeks earlier.

Geneva picked at the corners of her jelly-covered hoe cake. She'd slept well the night before, feeling safe for the first time in years. Yet, she dreaded the next two nights. She'd gone from taking care of her father in his drunken stupor most of the time to living with Hiriam in a loveless marriage. However, in all these experiences, she'd never spent a night alone. It couldn't be worse than the nights she'd spent with Hiriam, she'd told herself all morning but it hadn't worked. She absolutely dreaded going to sleep in her aunt's house without Reed there to keep her safe.

The soft rap on the door and a deep voice announcing that the taxi had arrived made them both jump. He stood up so fast the chair wobbled before it righted itself with a thud on the wooden floor. She pushed back her chair and was on her feet so rapidly that she blushed scarlet. They hadn't been doing anything except sharing breakfast, but she felt as if her thoughts had been spoken aloud and Reed had heard them, making her feel so foolish. After all, someone as big as she was shouldn't be afraid of anything the night could produce. Hadn't she spent half the night alone many times while she waited for her father to come home from the saloons?

They reached the door into the parlor at the same time and he stepped aside to let her go before him. She hesitated just a moment, turned back to tell him she would miss him, and suddenly he had her wrapped in his arms, their hearts keeping perfect time together. Using his fist, he tilted back her chin and closed his eyes, letting a strong magnetic force draw his lips to hers; tasting the sweet jelly on her breath; wishing he wasn't leaving; knowing he had to go. Knowing, too, that when he returned, things wouldn't have changed a bit. She wasn't interested in any man, most of all a Yankee.

She entwined her arms around his neck, her fingers sinking into his thick dark hair and holding on as if she could keep him forever and never have to watch him walk out the door. The kiss evoked the same feelings in her that the first one had done. A soft, spreading glow from the pits of her soul out to every nerve in her body. Nothing like she'd ever experienced before.

"I'm sorry. I promised. I gave my word that would

not happen again," he said hoarsely as he pulled away from her and picked up his valise from the rocking chair where he'd set it earlier.

"Don't apologize," she said.

He looked deeply into her blue eyes, a place where he could easily drown if he wasn't careful. A cool well of water beckoning to him to wade right in and experience a lifetime of kisses to shoot lightning bolts through his whole body. A forbidden place. She'd been a widow less than a month. For the next year she should be wearing black, not kissing a man whom she'd only met by accident.

"I'll see you in three days. Take care of Angelina and we'll talk when I get home," he was out the door before she could say another word.

She leaned into the open door jamb and watched him until the enclosed buggy disappeared into the misty, foggy morning. He'd said they'd talk when he got home. He'd actually used the word *home*. For a moment, the past was gone and the future looked bright. For barely a fraction of a second, time stood still. Then the warmth of the kiss on her lips faded and the loneliness quickly set in.

She'd donned the old dress that morning for a purpose, she reminded herself as she shut and locked the door. She was going to start all the way at the top of the house, in the dusty attic and systematically go through everything until there was no more time. In it, she hoped to find out as much as she could about her lost family and maybe as the lawyer Lawrence had suggested, take a few mementos to pass on to

Angelina. Because what came out of this house would be the only inheritance the child would ever have. What Hiriam might have left for her went up in smoke that day the house burned.

Angelina's eyes were open but she appeared to be quite content to lie on the bed, so Geneva opened the door from the bedroom to the attic and peered up the narrow, steep stairs. She'd be able to hear the baby if she even whimpered, but it was so dark up there, she'd have to light a lamp and take it with her. In the hour before the baby began to fuss, she found a treasure trove in an old trunk. A leather-bound picture album with a dozen tin types of her mother and Minnie as they grew up. A bundle of letters tied neatly with a pink bow addressed to Eva from someone named David O'Reilly. Geneva tucked them into her pocket and carried them down the dusty stairs.

Angelina had set up a real wail by the time she reached the bedside. Geneva removed the dusty apron, unbuttoned the bodice of her dress and nursed the baby while she untied the letters. Davie, as he signed his letters, was an Irish boy who'd worked on the next plantation over from the Edmonds' place. From what Geneva could ascertain he and Eva had met when she and her sister had been invited next door for a spring barbecue. Davie had been the horse trainer there, and he and Eva had fallen in love the first night they met. He'd written six letters in all, the last one begging her forgiveness. Her father, also his employer, had found out about their trysts and Davie had been fired. Her father had given him an ultimatum. If he ever tried to see Eva again, he'd have him shot and buried so far back in the woods, they'd never find his body. Or Mr. Edmonds would buy him a ticket on a stage to the nearest shipyard and from there he'd be booked passage back to Ireland to his family.

The last letter assured Eva that he would never forget her and that he would always love her. And that he was sending her a picture to remember him by. Water marks blurred the ink in several places. Geneva wondered if they were the result of Davie's tears or her mother's. Feeling restless after the baby was sleeping again, she paced around the room. There were other trunks in the attic she could prowl through, but how much more did she really want to know?

She picked up the silver brush from the dresser. Should she tuck that into her trunk, also? Did her mother ever brush her own hair with the brush? She turned it over and found it engraved with *E. E.* So it had belonged to her mother and not to Minnie after all. Geneva laid the brush beside the letters and the album. She fingered the picture on the dresser and finally took it from the frame so she could see it better. On the back, in faded handwriting, she read: *To my Eva, with all my love forever, Davie.*

She dropped it on the floor, and then retrieved it, taking a long look at the handsome young man on the front. Why had Minnie kept the brush and the picture? Why had she put them on the dresser? Geneva began to remove one object at a time until there was nothing left but the dresser scarf. She grabbed the corner of it and there underneath it was a letter, addressed to Eva Edmonds O'Grady.

With trembling hands she carried it to the chair and sunk down into it. She broke the wax seal on the back and opened it, unfolded the pages and gazed at the fine handwriting on the first page. Then she flipped to the back to find her aunt's signature. She held the letter to her chest for a few minutes before she began to read:

My dearest sister:

I know if you find the dresser like you left it in your bedroom on the plantation, you'll find this letter. I'm not going to live another week and I would have loved to have seen you one more time before the end, but there's a bond between us that has always been there and I know you will feel my death and come home to me. I left the money from the plantation to a college for women and also when I'm dead the money from the house will be left to that too. So if you've come home and are reading this, you'll probably already know that I left you the stock Daddy bought in that coal and navigation company on the East Coast. Also there are a couple of jars of very special jelly in the cupboard in the kitchen, back behind all the other jars. With the fall of the country in this horrendous war, I don't trust the banks. It will help you if you've still a mind to come back home and leave the tinker ways.

Geneva finished the letter then picked Angelina up and carried her downstairs to the kitchen. Sure enough, right there in the jelly cupboard, where she'd found the jelly that morning, were two quart jars filled with money. Tears ran down her cheeks as she counted out the bills. It staggered her that her aunt could wind that much money around inside the jars. She and Angelina would be fine. There was more than enough money to buy a wagon and go back to the tinker ways. Or to take her to New York.

She put the money back in the jars and hid them safely where they'd been for a long time. Did she want to raise her daughter in a wagon, rootless, free, going from place to place? Or did she want to buy a small house, invest part of the money, and give her roots and stability? It didn't take her long to abandon the idea of a wagon and give more thought to a home, maybe even one with azaleas in the yard and a tree where Angelina could have a swing.

Reed read a newspaper from cover to cover but had no idea what he'd read when he laid it aside. He watched the Virginia countryside speed past and got lost in his own thoughts. He'd been crazy to let his emotions carry him away and kiss Geneva again. True, it had him wondering the whole way from the house to the rail station if all kisses with her would come near to stopping his heart.

Then he drew himself up short and reminded himself that it didn't matter. There was no way Geneva would commit to another marriage, not after the shabby way she'd been treated. Besides he'd promised Indigo he wouldn't bring home a Southern woman like the other two boys had done. In her last letter she'd been railing against both Monroe and Rueben, saying that their wives were fine enough for Southern women, but they could have surely found someone just as fine from the right side of the war. He'd penned a note a few days before leaving Savannah in which he'd given her his promise that he would come home a bachelor and that he'd be sure to be there before her wedding in August.

The later promise wouldn't be so very hard to keep. After all, there were still a couple of weeks before the wedding. Three days from now he'd buy a horse and go north to Shirleysburg or else rely on trains and coaches to get him home. The first promise to come home a single man wouldn't be difficult either. After all, the timing wasn't right to marry Geneva even if he had a mind to ask her. His brothers might have found Southern wives and taken them home at the worst possible time in the world. But they weren't newly widowed with a new baby, and they hadn't been raised in a different culture like the tinkers, either. He sighed heavily. Why was he entertaining thoughts of marriage anyway? A month ago he was expertly dodging all women who had an itch to put a gold ring on their left hand.

"Looks like you have the weight of the world on your shoulders," a feminine voice said from the seat across the aisle.

Reed looked over into the softest light-green eyes

he'd ever seen. She wasn't a tall beauty like Geneva. Right the opposite. Rather plain in her gray traveling dress and matching hat, sitting straight on the top of light-brown hair twisted up at the nape of her neck in a bun.

"Just figuring things out," he said.

"Where are you going? Washington D.C.?" she asked.

"That's right. A quick turnaround trip. And you?" he asked.

"The same, and from there on to Philadelphia, Pennsylvania. I've been in Lynchburg to bring a cousin home with me," she nodded toward a matronly lady sleeping soundly in the seat beside her. "Dear old Cousin Prudence. She was married to a man who had slaves. When he died and they were freed, she was destitute, so my parents sent me to bring her to live with them. She was my mother's favorite cousin when they were growing up. I was wondering if I might borrow your newspaper if you are finished with it. I'm a school teacher in Philadelphia and it's been weeks since I've seen a paper. Trying to get Cousin Prudence's affairs in order so she could be moved, and everything."

"Of course," Reed handed her the paper. "Oh, I'm Harry Reed Hamilton of up near Shirleysburg. A little place called Love's Valley."

"Well, it's nice to meet you Mr. Hamilton. I'm Georganna Wilson of Philadelphia. And I'm really grateful to you for the use of your newspaper. It's a boring trip at best and I'm afraid Cousin Prudence doesn't provide much company," she smiled.

Reed didn't need a signed document from President Johnson to know she was flirting. She was from his part of the world. A responsible woman who had an education. Her fingertips had lingered on his when she reached for the paper, but they'd caused no fire to heat up his insides like a touch from Geneva.

"You are very welcome," he said and went back to staring out the window. Flirting or not, he wasn't in the mood to allow another woman into his thoughts. Not until he'd figured out what he was going to do with Geneva. Not even if Georganna persisted, which she wouldn't. An upstanding school teacher woman would know when she was being given a cold shoulder, wouldn't she?

Across the street from Geneva's temporary dwelling a lanky man sat on a board sidewalk and watched the lamplight go from the top floor down to the bottom one. He wore his trousers tucked down into a pair of custom-made deep red boots, and a sweat-stained work shirt covered with a leather vest. Geneva O'Grady Garner was in that house. The man had left with a valise so he'd be gone a few days. He'd heard that the two of them visited a lawyer yesterday and then went straight to the house. Geneva had been carrying a baby in her arms so somewhere along the way she'd had the child. Hiriam's baby.

The sheriff of Savannah had said he wanted the

baby and her both dead, their bodies photographed and brought to him. Then he'd pay five hundred dollars when he had the pictures in his hands. He didn't care to have the bodies shipped back to Savannah. No, that would be a stinking mess because it would take weeks. Just hire a photographer to take pictures of them dead and that would do, along with any kind of paper stating that the deceased was indeed Geneva O'Grady Garner and that the baby was hers. That would free the land to be sold at auction.

The man lit a cigar and drew smoke deeply into his lungs. He had a couple of days from what he'd found out already. There was no hurry. He might even wait until the last day before the man came back to the house. Then Mr. Reed Hamilton, Yankee Major himself, could be the ones to find the bodies. That would be justice for helping the tinker woman escape. Most likely they'd had something going on for months. The child might not even be Hiriam's. The man drew on the cigar and contemplated how he'd take care of the situation. Hanging was what she deserved. What the Klan would prefer. But it wouldn't work here, and not with the baby. Even the Klan couldn't get away with stringing up an infant. No, it would have to be with a bullet, or maybe a pillow and suffocation for the baby.

He'd told the sheriff that they could simply go to the Lynchburg sheriff's office and provide a warrant for her arrest then he could ride away with the mother and baby tied to a horse behind him. After all, she was wanted for murder and arson back in Georgia. Along the way he could make sure they ended up dead. Mayhap he could even do a hanging if they were out away from a town. But the sheriff had decided to do it differently and he was the boss. Both of Savannah and the Klan.

Now all the sheriff's deputy had to do was decide which was the least messy way to clean up the sheriff's stupid mistake. If he'd searched the place a little better, they'd have found her. The Savannah station manager had finally admitted a big, dirty woman who smelled like a smoke stack had bought a ticket to Ridgeland. The sheriff had had business up there and didn't find her, but he'd sent the deputy. The path hadn't been hard to follow. Maybe the deputy should be the boss of the Klan. He smiled at that idea.

So what would it be? Bullet. Garrote. Knife. It would depend on whether there was thunder to cover the noise of the gun, or if it was a still night with no sounds. Then the knife might be the choice weapon. For now, he'd just watch the house and keep her under surveillance.

Chapter Fourteen

"Reed Hamilton, how good to see you," President Johnson stood up from behind his massive desk and extended his hand.

Reed shook the offered hand and slid a sheaf of papers across the desk at the same time. "There is my report. Nearly two years worth of what I've investigated."

"And I'm sure it's correct. Have a seat. We'll have lunch in a little while but first we'll discuss the South. Now tell me, you've had your fingers on the pulse of the country down there. What did you discover? I know it's in the report, but summarize it very briefly for me," the President said.

"The Klan is getting stronger and stronger. What started out as a prank with a few men acting silly has become a terror. The sheriff of Savannah is in on it. I came on that bit of information as I was leaving. Let me tell you the story," he said and related to the President of the United States the whole tale from the time he left Savannah until he and Geneva reached Lynchburg.

The President listened intently. "I offered Monroe a position in the government. We need men like the Hamiltons working for us. I'd like to offer you the same. Although with the unrest in the White House right now, I wouldn't blame you if you turned me down cold. One vote in the impeachment business was all that kept me in office. I won't be elected again, I'm sure, and I can't say as it bothers me. The radicals are setting the Southern states back years with the laws and restrictions they've enforced."

"I've been a spy long enough, sir. I'm ready to go home to Love's Valley and settle down. I thank you for the offer and for the trust you put in me," Reed said.

"Going to settle down with the young lady you rescued?" the President asked with a twinkle in his eyes.

"Been asking myself the same question the past twenty-four hours. I don't think so. I don't know. It's a complicated affair. She's only been widowed a few weeks, but again, it was a loveless marriage. A royal mess, I'm afraid. But I would like to ask a tremendous favor. I'd like a paper stating that she is not wanted for murder and arson," Reed said.

"Done," the President said. "It'll be ready for you to pick up after we have lunch. I hope you don't mind but Martha has invited a friend for lunch. She's a distant cousin of Martha's husband and the two of them became fast friends when my daughter married into the family."

"Thank you and no, I do not mind," Reed said. "It will be a delight to see Martha again. And how does Mrs. Johnson fare these days?"

"The same. Nothing changes much in that part of my life," the President said forlornly. "I'm just thankful Martha helps out as much as she does."

A valet appeared to inform them that lunch was being served in the dining room. Reed and President Johnson followed him down the stairs to the big room where a small table had been set up in front of long windows. Drapes had been tied back. The reflection of sun rays normally would have danced across the highly polished floor, but only the gray skies and heavy rain were visible.

"Reed, how delightful to see you again," Martha said when she heard the door open.

"Same here. How's the family?" Reed smiled.

"We're all fine," she said. "I'd like you to meet my dear friend, Georganna Wilson. She's a distant cousin."

"So we meet again?" Georganna extended her hand.

It fit well in Reed's big hand but her shake was limp. Not at all like he imagined Geneva's would be. "What a nice surprise," he said, the corners of his mouth turning up in what Indigo called his fake grin.

"Yes, it is," Georganna said. "We met on the train from Lynchburg, Martha. Mr. Hamilton was kind enough to share his newspaper with me or I'm sure I would have perished from acute boredom."

Martha laughed and showed them to their seats.

Nothing could have been better. She didn't believe for one minute in fate or destiny or any of those things, but Georganna had just been telling her about this handsome man she'd met on the train and how much she'd like to get to know him better. She'd been about to tell her the man's name when the President arrived with Reed. Coincidence was what it was, but Martha would play it for all it was worth. The Hamiltons were the backbone of the North. They'd supported the war financially but more importantly with their lives. All three Hamilton men had gone beyond their duty when her father asked them to do an extended enlistment to help with the reconstruction. Actually, it was just a cover for them to spy on the actual happenings and to report to the President with the news. She wondered what Reed had brought, but she'd never know. The report would be stamped with a confidential seal and her father would be the only one who'd ever read it.

"I've ordered sugar cured ham," Martha said after they were seated. "I seem to remember that it's a favorite of yours, Reed." She didn't tell him that she kept files on everyone who'd ever been in the White House, what they liked, what they'd pushed aside and hadn't touched.

"How nice of you to remember something like that. Yes, it is my favorite. And I bet you have candied yams and fresh green beans?" Reed grinned for real.

"Exactly," Martha said as they were served the lunch.

"Now tell us about what's going on in Philadelphia," the President said to Georganna.

"Well, as you know we say we're from Philadelphia but actually we live in Douglass in Berks County. The people there have realized the importance of water-works and have built several mills along Iron Stone Creek. Wren's Wooling Mill is doing well. Also the Coalbrookdale Iron Works that makes cast iron cooking stoves, sadirons and wash kettles has just been sold this year to Brendlinger and Company. So it's business as usual. My school is faring very well. We have more than a hundred children now. Several teachers and we're considering keeping it open more than six months next year," she said, hoping to impress Reed. Good grief, to think the man was one of the President's friends. It would indeed be a feather in her cap to have him come calling.

"Have you ever heard of the LeHigh Coal and Navigation Company?" Reed asked, thoroughly enjoying the ham.

"Oh, yes," the President said. "It's well known in these parts. Brings coal down from New York to the Philadelphia area."

"I've heard tell that it will probably be undergoing some changes," Georganna said, nibbling at the ham, which was certainly not her favorite main course. "There are rumors on the wind that it may be converting to using railroad cars in the near future instead of barges."

"Oh, then it did survive the war?" Reed asked.

"Yes, it surely did. After all, we do have to keep warm and coal is what we use," Georganna gave him her best smile.

"Do the Hamiltons have an interest in the coal and navigation company?" the President asked.

"No, but the name came across my desk awhile back," Reed filled his mouth with candied yams to keep from having to answer any more questions right away. So Geneva had an interest in a thriving company. More than likely it would be enough to keep her and Angelina at least modestly in New York. A sharp needle of pain passed through his heart. She wouldn't need him once he told her about the business, and he'd have to tell her, because even if that's all she was, she was his friend.

Somehow he said the right things through the rest of lunch and said the proper thank yous for everything before he left the White House, papers in hand that said Geneva O'Grady Garner was not responsible for the hanging of her husband or the burning of his plantation. It also stated that if there were no other relatives that the plantation would be Geneva's to hold in trust for her child until the child reached the age of twenty-one. That was surely an added bonus, Reed thought as he stepped out of the cab the President had sent him back to the hotel in. Now if she wanted, she could even go back to Savannah a free woman with land where she could build a new house.

"Well, my, my," a feminine voice said from the lobby of the hotel. "We are surely thrown together often, aren't we, Mr. Hamilton?"

"Seems that way," Reed suddenly felt claustrophobic. As if he were being fenced in with that new barbed wire he'd read about. "It's nice to see you again, Miss Wilson. I had no idea we were staying at the same hotel. We could have used the same cab." *But thank goodness I didn't know,* he thought.

"Yes, we could have," she brightened. "I'm planning on seeing some sights this afternoon. Would your plans permit you to escort me? I know that's a bit forward and before the war I would have been horrified to even suggest such a thing but times have changed and I would like to visit with you more."

"It would have been a pleasure, but I'm afraid I have pressing business the rest of the afternoon and then tomorrow morning I'll be on the early train back to Lynchburg," he lied, his conscience as clear as a spring morning in Love's Valley. Survival. The woman had invisible barbed wire in her hands and dollar signs engraved on her forehead. Martha had no doubt told her all about the Hamiltons. He'd seen that look many, many times and had become quite adept at getting out of close calls.

"Well then, until later. I'm in room three-fourteen if you change your mind or if you'd like company for dinner this evening. Cousin Prudence and I will be having dinner in the dining room at six sharp. We'd love to see you there," she said.

"We shall see how much business I can accomplish this afternoon," he said woefully, almost believable even to himself.

As soon as he was in his room, he removed his waistcoat, vest and tie, changed into a more comfortable suit and caught a valet in the hallway. "Would you please send someone to the train station and ask if there is anything going to Lynchburg before morning?"

An hour later the news came that there was indeed a late train going that way. It would be leaving at five-thirty and arriving early the next morning. Reed sent the boy to purchase a ticket, with instructions to leave it at the front desk and have a cab ready to take him to the station at four-thirty. The Wilson women would be getting ready for dinner at that hour so he could avoid another situation. Then he stretched out on the bed and fell asleep, only to dream of a man in a white sheet and hood over his head, chasing after Geneva, who kept yelling his name. Reed's shoes were so heavy he could barely run toward her. He grabbed his gun from the shoulder holster but the bullets he shot at the man were moving so slow they'd never catch up with him before he grabbed Geneva and the baby.

Geneva sent a young boy who'd been playing on the sidewalk to the lawyer's office with a note inviting him to tea that afternoon at two o'clock. When the boy returned with the word from Mr. Lawrence that he would be free to visit at that time, she busied herself getting ready to walk to town and purchase the things she needed to make a proper tea for a lawyer. She and Angelina bought a loaf of bread and four kinds of cookies from the bakery on the main street of town. She bought thin-sliced country cured ham and half a pound of pork sausage seasoned with sage from the butcher's shop. She'd cook the ham quickly in an iron skillet and serve it on the fresh bread. Then she bought a pound of cheese which she planned to grate, then add to the sausage along with flour and leavening. Half an hour in the oven and she'd have tasty little sausage tidbits. A quick turnaround in the general store produced a good grade of tea and a quarter pound of coffee. If the portly Mr. Lawrence didn't eat everything, she'd nibble on the rest for supper.

"Just one more day," she talked to herself as she walked home to wait for the delivery of her purchases. *I'm going to ask him to take me with him to Love's Valley and from there I'll go on to New York to live,* she decided as she walked. She didn't like life without Reed Hamilton in it, and she was big enough to admit it to herself. To admit it to him was another thing altogether, but another week with the knowledge would give her time to either build her courage or figure out she'd only had a case of loneliness. Either way, by then she'd know her heart for sure.

The rain had stopped mid-morning and the humidity was enough to smother her to death. Especially in the dark blue traveling suit which she'd washed yesterday after Reed left. Lot of good it did. She'd carefully washed it and rinsed it until it was fresh and clean. Didn't wring it at all to keep the wrinkles at bay and spent more than an hour with the flat irons after it dried. All for naught. Because sweat ran down her neck and between her breasts. By the time she reached the house the suit would be as sour as it had been before it was washed. She'd have to change into the pale blue dress for the tea. Open all the windows and hopefully a breeze would kick up. Right then though she didn't think there was any wind between Lynchburg and Savannah. One couldn't be bought, borrowed, stolen, or even cussed up. The stillness laden with humidity brought out the sweat, beading upon her upper lip as well as making the rest of her body feel like it had been rolled in sweet sugar syrup. Yet in the midst of it all she shivered. A cold aura surrounded her. Doom breathed down its icy wind into her soul. Something was wrong. Definitely amiss.

Was it Reed? Had he been killed? *No,* she walked slower. The sensation of cold fingers reached into her heart and squeezed, making her shudder again. It wasn't Reed in trouble; it was herself and Angelina. She could feel it deep in her bones, as surely as the Tuatha'an soothsayer, who told fortunes often in the winter when they were camped. Old Molly said she could feel things amiss in her bones, and Geneva could at that moment. It was as clear as a summer day with no clouds in the sky. Something was definitely wrong. She glanced over her shoulder. No one back there. Ahead of her. Just a bunch of little boys playing kickball up and down the street. Across the street stood a man, tall, lanky, wearing a gun, hat shoved down over his face. She walked faster. So did he. She walked slower. So did he. Her hands were shaking so badly when she opened the door to her aunt's house that she feared she would drop the baby.

She went straight up the stairs and peeped out the bedroom window. The man had sat down on the sidewalk across the street and lit up a cigar. She shut her eyes tightly. A vision of the sheriff and two other men riding up to the plantation, robes flapping, hoods hiding their faces. All that was visible were their evil eyes and boots. The sheriff in his highly polished black boots. The mayor in matching ones. The other man in dark red tooled boots that he wore with his trousers tucked deep inside.

"Baby girl, I think the long arm of the sheriff does reach this far. I wonder what that man has in mind for us. If he was going to arrest us and take us to the sheriff in this town he would have already done so. So that leaves the only other alternative." She sat down in the rocking chair and made herself breathe. She might be shot or killed, but she'd go down fighting like a tiger for her child.

"Know thy enemy," the memory of her father's voice whispered softly in her mind. "You can't defeat the enemy and win the war if you don't know who you are fighting against."

"I know that daddy, and I will fight the battle. But all I know about him is that he's sitting across the street puffing on a cigar and wearing red boots," she said aloud. "Maybe Reed will be home before the fighting begins. I surely hope so."

Chapter Fifteen

Geneva and the lawyer had tea but she learned precious little more about her mother. Mr. Lawrence wanted to talk about himself more than he did about the Edmonds family. She had the idea by the middle of the hour that he was trying to impress her with his accomplishments and all he owned; that if she would give him a half a chance he would propose to her right there in the parlor as he gorged himself on sausage tidbits and ham sandwiches. He'd even told her that if she wanted to stay in Lynchburg he was sure he knew just the right little house she could purchase. It was only a few doors down from his townhouse. Of course, he still had the family plantation and he'd be glad to show it to her anytime she wanted a refreshing ride in the country.

"Whew!" She leaned against the door jamb when he was finally gone, "Come home, Reed," she mumbled. She glanced out the door to find the man still watching her house. Perhaps she should have mentioned it to the lawyer, but it was a free world and there was more than one man sitting on the sidewalk. The only difference was that the others seemed to stay awhile and then go on. None of them had taken up squatter's rights right across the street from her house.

Surely he wouldn't do anything in broad daylight. Not without a white robe and hood, anyway. Maybe he was just waiting for the sheriff to reach Lynchburg from Savannah or maybe he was the watchdog for another group of cowardly men who'd organized in the state of Virginia. Her imagination ran wild with different scenarios.

"Nothing will happen," she kept telling herself as she climbed the stairs and took Angelina back to the bedroom where she could keep an eye on the man from the upstairs window.

At dusk he still sat there. She prepared for bed, assuring herself all the time that nothing would happen. Surely more than one man in the South had a pair of boots that color and lots of men wore their pants tucked down inside the tops of them. She put fresh sheets she'd found in her aunt's dresser drawer on the bed and fluffed up several feather pillows after she'd stuffed them down into embroidered pillowcases. She wondered if she'd be stretching her rights to take a couple pairs of the cases in which her mother's initials were embroidered in the corners.

She shut the door carefully, wiring the inside to a nail which had been hammered in about halfway, and

then she and Angelina went to bed. She was completely worn-out from the afternoon's work but she couldn't
sleep. And she wasn't at all surprised when she heard
the window sash squeak slightly in the bedroom.

"Shhh," Deputy Jack Dally said under his breath as
he slipped into the bedroom where the light had gone
out earlier that evening. Stupid woman hadn't even
known he'd been watching her for two whole days.
There she was resting easy under the blankets, a
smaller figure lying right beside her. It was going to be
an easy job after all. It would be the easiest five hundred dollars Jack Dally ever made in his life. When
the sheriff paid him, he had a notion he might go to
California. Even if the first rush for gold was long
since over, he might do a little panning just for fun.

No breeze fluttered the curtains out into the room.
No thunder rolled to cover gun shots, so Jack had
decided to use the knife. It really wasn't his weapon of
choice. He preferred the neat, easy bullet. Shoot 'em
and leave 'em. If the Klan would adopt the gun over
the rope, he'd happy to do all their killings for them,
though he didn't see that happening. They loved the
rope and the lesson it left behind with a corpse hanging from a tree saying they were in charge. But in
Lynchburg, Virginia, far away from Savannah,
Georgia, Jack Dally was the boss and he wasn't using
a rope or a gun. No sir. To hang that big woman in her
own house could very well be too much job for a man
of Jack's stature. A gun would make noise which
could bring out the next door neighbor or at the least

it would open the possibility of someone seeing him. He'd been so sly up until now; he wasn't going to risk being caught.

He unsheathed a ten-inch fillet knife from its leather home in his belt. First the woman and then the baby. If he did the baby first, the woman would awaken and give him a tussle. Big as that lady was, he didn't want a fight on his hands. No sir, she might mark his face with her fingernails and then he'd have some explaining to do.

Geneva lay still and held her breath. At least Angelina was sleeping soundly. Maybe she was hearing things in her fear, she attempted to tell herself, but when the man chuckled she knew he was in the bedroom.

Using both hands, Jack raised the knife high above his head and brought it down with as much force as he could muster. Right where he figured her heart would be. Pierce that and she'd be dead before she could open her eyes. He brought the knife from her body as fast as he'd slammed it into her breast. A dark substance covered the blade and she didn't move, but he wasn't taking any chances. The sheriff said to make sure she was dead, so he counted them out silently as he stabbed the woman ten times. Blood covered the sheet she'd used to cover up her body and face. He had no desire to rip the sheet back and see the look on her face. Dead people held no fascination for Jack. No sir. He did his job and did it well, but he didn't have to look at the lovely woman to know she was dead. Her face was probably just as beautiful as it had been when she was breathing. She would have never known what hit her if the knife had indeed found its mark on the first try.

He heard a slight whimper. The kid was waking. He didn't want to kill a tiny baby unless it was asleep so he ran around the bed, his boots making enough noise to wake the neighbors if their windows were open, and quickly stabbed the baby. He was glad sheets covered the child because he'd never killed a baby before. A pang of guilt struck him in the chest but it didn't last long. Five hundred dollars was a lot of money and the sheriff would be glad to know the Garner farm could be bought for taxes next year.

He carefully wiped the dark substance from the knife blade on the window curtain and slipped back out into the deep shadows provided by a moonless, cloudy night and lots of shade trees around the house. Tomorrow when the bodies were discovered he'd collect the photographs he'd already paid a man to take and his job would be done. When they were in his pocket, he'd light a shuck for Savannah.

Reed wished the train would go faster. The dream he'd had about Geneva gave him cold chills in spite of the sticky, hot night air. He tried closing his eyes but that didn't work. He tried thinking of Love's Valley, of Indigo and her wedding to Thomas. That didn't work either. Finally he got up and paced the length of the train. Very few passengers traveled at night and those who did were sleeping soundly, some snoring loudly.

When the train finally came to a halt in Lynchburg,

every nerve in his body was taut. Something was terribly wrong. He'd relied on his sixth sense in his work for years and it had never failed him. Either Geneva was in danger or there was something horrible going on in Love's Valley. Only his family could work his extra senses to the extent that he became nauseous. Family? But Geneva wasn't family. She was barely even his friend.

And if you believe that, you are crazy, his conscience told him bluntly.

A big orange sliver of light appeared through the trees, bringing dawn and sunlight, but Reed's heart was as black as midnight. If Geneva had been hurt, the culprit better spend the rest of his life on his knees getting right with God. He looked around for a cab but there were none to be had at that early morning hour, so he set a course across town to Aunt Minnie's house.

Everything looked normal when he turned the corner and saw the house. But the veil of apprehension still covered him from head to foot. He wouldn't rest easy until he found her and Angelina safe and sound. Maybe she'd even be in the kitchen cooking breakfast. He stopped on the porch. Should he knock? If she was sleeping still, that would awaken her. If he didn't knock, then he could slip inside and perhaps have breakfast ready for her when she came down the stairs. That would be a nice surprise.

He turned the knob and found the door unlocked. Blasted woman. Didn't she know enough about living in a city to lock the door at night? All kinds of riffraff roamed the streets since the end of the war. A woman alone in the house would be easy prey for any of them.

He checked the kitchen. The stove was cold. He peeked under a tablecloth to find the leftovers from supper. Cookies, a quarter loaf of bread, some kind of little round balls. Tea. She'd had tea with the lawyer and these were the leftovers. He tiptoed carefully up the stairs and peeked into the room he'd used, dropping his valise on the bed. Everything was the same. Her bedroom door was slightly ajar so he peeped inside, expecting to see her curled up around Angelina, the two of them still sleeping. The sight on the bed brought on both rage and weak knees. There was no doubt what had happened. The window curtain belled out with the fresh morning breeze and the dark stuff all over the bed was on the lacy curtain, too.

"No, no!" he bellowed, shoving the door open and standing before the bed. She was gone and he'd never told her that he'd fallen in love with her. Now it was too late. Too late to admit that she'd laid claim to his heart. In the half light of the early morning, Reed Hamilton wept.

"Geneva, I'm so sorry," he moaned as he sunk into the rocking chair. "I'm so so sorry. I should've stayed. I should have taken you with me."

A movement on the other side of the room caught his eye and suddenly the attic door swung open and there was Geneva in her nightdress, holding Angelina tightly to her breast. "Reed, you're home early. What's the matter? Why are you crying?" she asked

then saw the mess on the bed and her knees went
weak. She felt herself falling and then being gathered
up by a pair of strong arms, supporting her and the
baby.

"What happened?" he asked, carrying both of them
downstairs to the parlor. "Who is that in your bed?"

Geneva shook the sticky cobwebs from her brain.
Reed had been weeping. Crying because he thought
she was dead. She needed to think all that through
carefully. "Put me down. You'll break your back. I'm
not a willow-o-the-wisp. Set me in the rocker and I'll
tell you all about it," she said, uncovering Angelina
from her blanket to make sure she was all right and
hadn't hit the floor when Geneva came too almighty
close to fainting.

"Are you sure you're all right? Do I need to call a
doctor? You're not hurt? Who is that up there dead in
your bed?" Reed asked questions so fast her ears hurt
from them.

"I'm fine, Reed. Angelina is fine. There's no one in
the bed. Just hear me out and let me tell you what's
happened. The deputy from Savannah was watching
the house when you were away. Sitting over there on
the sidewalk across the street, and following me to the
store when I went to buy things for the tea with the
lawyer. I knew it was him because I recognized his red
boots and the way he wears his trousers tucked down
into them. Daddy used to tell me to know the enemy,
to think like he would, or I'd never outsmart the old
wolf. I felt like the wolf was scratching at my soul and
I was so cold, Reed. I knew he'd make his move under

the cover of night. I sat in this chair and tried to think evil thoughts like him and that sheriff. I wished for you to come home, to be here with us. I was terrified. But I made myself think like he would. He'd either shoot me or stab me. He couldn't risk a hanging like the Klan usually does. Especially with a baby. It was a still night and a gunshot would carry, so I figured he'd use a knife. I left the door open on purpose but he crawled up onto the porch roof and came in through the window. There was an old dress form up in the attic. Not so very different from my size. I used it under the sheets and fashioned a head for it from a pillowcase, which I covered with dust cap and made it look like I'd covered my face with the sheet. Then I made a form about Angelina's size and put it under the sheet."

"But the blood?" he said, his mind still reeling from seeing her there, afraid he really was seeing an apparition in his grief.

"Jelly. Lots of it. Plum jelly. I covered up that dress form in it, and then carefully laid a cloth over it before I covered it all up with the sheet. He needed to think he was seeing blood, didn't he? If he'd drawn that knife out and it was clean, he would have come looking all over the house for me," she said.

Reed threw back his head and laughed, easing some of the tension from his shoulders and soul. "Would you like to work for the government as a spy?" he asked.

"Is that what you are?" she asked wide eyed.

"Not anymore," he said. "Now what are we going to do?"

"Hang the sheriff's deputy with his own rope. I did have one terrible moment. Mostly, I just stayed very quiet on that old bed up in the attic. But I could hear him grunting with the force of the blows and about that time Angelina woke up and whimpered. I was terrified that he'd hear her up in the attic. I heard him leaving awhile later and I didn't sleep all night but we didn't come down until I heard your voice. I'm sorry I scared you so badly, but I did the best I could," she said.

He wanted to gather her in his arms again, but suddenly he was tongue-tied and shy. He loved the woman but she'd only lost her husband a month before. That there was no love in the marriage didn't matter, it was still too soon.

"Like I said, we'll use his rope and hang him with it. Go to the sheriff and tell him what's happened. Bring him and the funeral man back with you. A covered hearse would be a nice touch. You can take the bodies down to the hearse and to the funeral place. If you and the sheriff pretend they're about as heavy as me and the baby would be and keep them wrapped in the sheets with just enough jelly showing to make them look real, it would be convincing. I'm sure he's hiding somewhere right now, waiting to see what happens next. I'm willing to bet he has to take back proof. He'll have a photographer come and take pictures of the bodies like they do outlaws," Geneva said.

"Yes, ma'am, President Johnson would hire you in a minute," Reed said through an orange-sized lump still in his throat.

"Go out with your head hanging low as if you really cared about me," she said. "If the deputy is watching, he'll expect that."

And if it had been you in that bed, it wouldn't be an act, he thought as he nodded in agreement.

"If we can catch this man, I'm sure the President would just love to have him interrogated. He's sending in men to take care of the Klan in Savannah this week. What that deputy could tell him would sure help," Reed said.

"Oh, we'll catch him. He's not very bright," Geneva said. "Now I think I'll have some breakfast from yesterday's leftovers while you go get the right folks to haul my jelly-covered body out of here."

"I've got lots to tell you when I get back," he touched her shoulder and looked down into the wide open eyes of the baby girl he'd helped bring into the world. "Don't go near the windows or the doors. Our murderer doesn't need to see ghosts."

"Oh, he's going to see ghosts all right. He's going to see lots of them in the last few minutes before he dies. They say the past comes back to haunt you and I bet he sees so many ghosts that he may die of fright rather than a broken neck or suffocation," Geneva said stoically. Just the touch of Reed's fingertips on her shoulders had caused that same warm feeling in the pit of her stomach. She'd decided during the night in the attic that she was going to tell him exactly how he affected her. But doing it wasn't going to be easy. Just because she'd outwitted a killer did not mean she'd changed. She was still a tinker's daughter. Still a widow who should be wearing widow's weeds instead of gay colored blue dresses. Still a Southern woman and Reed had no interest in Southern women.

But if she didn't speak her mind, she'd never forgive herself. At least she had a couple of weeks to work up the nerve to tell him before they got to Love's Valley.

Chapter Sixteen

"It's over," Reed leaned against the bedroom door jamb and looked down on Geneva rocking Angelina to sleep. "It all went down just like you said. The photographer came with his equipment to take pictures of the bodies. He gave up the name of the deputy without a fight, saying he didn't want any trouble. The sheriff nabbed Jack Dally when he came to pick up his pictures. He's already in leg irons and being escorted by train to Washington D. C. tonight. He'll be interrogated and the information they get will help put the sheriff and mayor behind bars finally."

"Then it is really over," she said.

"And I brought papers that say you're not responsible too," he said. "We've got some other things to discuss, though."

"Have a seat, Reed," she smiled, her beautiful

face lighting up the room even more than the late afternoon sunlight flooding through the bedroom window.

He pulled a straight-back chair from the end of the dresser and placed it a few feet from the rocking chair. "I found out the LeHigh Coal and Navigation Company, the one that you've got an interest in, is a thriving business. It survived the war and is doing well. So you're not destitute."

"And Aunt Minnie left my mother a letter hiding under the dresser scarf over there," she said. "There's quite a lot of money in two jelly jars down in the kitchen that she left for my mother should she come back. Aunt Minnie thought Mother would feel in her heart that Minnie was dying and would come home. Little did she know that Mother beat her to heaven by a few years. So anyway, there's money down there that is my inheritance too."

"One more thing," Reed added. "I have papers saying that the plantation in Savannah is to be Angelina's, with you acting in her benefit until she comes of age. You can sell it or go back there," he said, holding his breath for her answer to that bit of news.

"I left nothing in Savannah I want to go back for. I'll sell it and put the money into a trust fund for Angelina, though I don't know how to go about it," she said.

"My lawyers could take care of that for you," he offered, his heart lighter just knowing she didn't want to go back south.

She fidgeted in the rocker. She should tell him how she felt but suddenly she was as tongue-tied as a little girl in a room full of boys. "Reed . . ."

"Geneva . . ."

They both started at once in a nervous voice.

"You go first," he totally expected her to say that she'd proven she could take care of herself and didn't need him anymore. That he'd fulfilled his part of the bargain made in the heat of fear when the wild boar almost killed Angelina.

"No, you finish," she demurred, not sure how to word what she wanted to tell him anyway. Not even sure now that it was over that the feeling in her heart hadn't been the byproduct of a terrible scare. Seeing where that horrid man had stabbed what he thought to be her and Angelina under the covers had sent her mind reeling. She really needed a few days just to collect her thoughts and figure out if she really did like this impossible Yankee, the most unlikely candidate in the entire world, from either North or South, for her to have feelings for.

"I don't think you and Angelina should stay here. I think you should go on to New York and see about that business with the company you have an interest in. I'd be glad to keep traveling with you up to Love's Valley and from near there you could get a train to New York," he blurted out.

"I'd like that. I thought about buying a tinker's wagon with the money from the jars and going back to the only thing I know how to do. I'm not afraid of the work or the loneliness but I'd like to give Angelina roots. You can't get those living among the Tuatha'an," she said.

Reed grinned. So she'd decided to go to New York. Not if he had his way about it. If she wanted roots for Angelina he knew the best ground in the whole world to put them down in. She could buy a small house in Shirleysburg, less than three miles from Love's Valley, live out her year in mourning and he could come and visit whenever he wanted. That would give them both time; Geneva, to see if she really was going to be a widow the rest of her life; himself, time to explore the feelings he'd come to recognize as more than friendship. Yes, sir, everything was working out just fine.

She waited for him to wipe the silly grin off his face and say something. Anything at all.

"I'm glad you're thinking of a permanent place for you and the baby," he finally told her.

"So when do we leave?" she asked.

"How about tonight? I'll book us a car to Washington and from there we'll have to take stages the rest of the way."

"That would be wonderful. I'd just as soon not stay another night in this house. I've picked out a few things that belonged to my mother and they're already in my trunk," she patted Angelina's back as she rocked.

"Then I'll go make the arrangements and be back in an hour," he touched her shoulder briefly and disappeared back down the stairs.

In the hour he was gone, Geneva carefully shut all the windows, made sure the kitchen cookstove was cold and all the embers dead inside. She retrieved the money from the jars and stashed it in the bottom of the baby's traveling valise. She dressed in the light blue dress, leaving her old worn calico draped across the back of the chair in the bedroom. The new owners could use it for mop rags or dusting cloths. She was finished with it and what it symbolized.

When Reed returned with a hack to take them to the train station, she was waiting on the porch. She handed him the skeleton key and he locked the door. She didn't even look back when they drove to the lawyer's office to return the key. She'd learned that her family didn't have halos and wings; neither did they have long forked tails and pitchforks. They were just people. She'd be willing to bet her grandparents died regretting the decisions they'd made that lost them their daughter. That the young man named Davie always remembered his decision not to fight for the love of his life, but scooted right back home when he met with opposition. She bore no resentment to any of them because it had taken both her mother and her father to make her the person she was and for the first time in Geneva's life, she liked herself.

The train car wasn't nearly as plush inside as the first one they'd ridden, but it was much nicer than sitting on a hard seat all night and trying to sleep propped up in a corner. It sure beat a bouncing stagecoach. How on earth Reed could ride in a stage and not get sick, yet couldn't ride on a ship without getting ill, was a complete enigma to Geneva. A ship sailing through the water had to be smoother than a four-wheeled contraption that hit every gopher and mole hole in the road.

She laid the baby in one of the two beds in the train car and removed her hat. Supper would be served in an hour and Reed had already claimed one of the stuffed chairs and had his nose in a newspaper. She pulled back the drapes just as the train began to move. The sun was still a bright orange ball but it wouldn't hang there in the sky much longer. Reed snored and startled her. So he hadn't slept too well last night either. A trip to Washington and back in less than forty-eight hours, it was no wonder. She sat down in the other chair and removed her shoes and stockings, letting her toes wiggle in freedom. In a few minutes she was asleep also.

Reed awoke with a start, shoving the newspaper from his face, grabbing for his gun. A quick survey of the moving car assured him he'd only been dreaming again. Angelina had kicked off her cover and was cooing at the ceiling. Geneva's head was laid over on the wing of the chair, her bare feet shining from under the skirt tail, and she was sleeping soundly. A knock on the door of the car let him know supper had arrived and reassured him that the first rap was probably what had awakened him.

He opened the door cautiously, his gun drawn. What he hadn't told Geneva was that Jack Dally was riding in a barred car with a deputy from Lynchburg.

His hands were cuffed to the bars and he wore leg irons, but until they reached Washington, D. C., Reed wouldn't totally be at ease.

"Supper," the steward said and rolled in a cart.

"Food?" Geneva roused up from her nap. "I'm starved."

"Right here okay?" the steward asked as he pushed the cart toward her chair.

"That will be fine," Reed said.

"I'll be back to collect the cart in an hour," the steward said. "Anything else you'd like to order to be delivered at that time?"

"Yes, a plate of fruit and one of sandwiches for a midnight snack if we should get hungry again. And a fresh carafe of coffee and one of tea," Reed said.

The steward wrote the order on a paper he fetched from his pocket and shut the door as Reed and Geneva began to uncover the dishes set before them. Fried chicken, potatoes in white sauce, small peas and a whole loaf of still-warm bread. A cherry pie and a tray of pastries for dessert.

"Heaven," Geneva tore off a chunk of bread and sopped up some of the sauce. "Ah, this is wonderful. Can we just ride the train the whole way to New York?"

"I don't think so," Reed bit into one of the crispy chicken legs on his plate. "From Washington, we can catch another train to Harrisburg, Pennsylvania. Then it will be stagecoaches. If everything connects and we don't have to stay in one town more than a day, it's a four-or five-day trip from there."

"One week. I thought you mentioned two weeks." Her courage faltered. She'd figured on longer to sort out her feelings.

"A little more than a week. In Washington, we may have to wait a day or so to get a train with a car to get us to Harrisburg. That's more than a hundred and fifty miles so it'll be a couple of days on the train. I'd rather have a private car for you and the baby and if it takes a couple of days, it would be worth it. Maybe we could see some sights while we're there. I'm sure the President would be glad to have us for lunch," he said.

"Oh, no, just thinking of that gives me hives," she laughed. "You're the spy, not me. I wouldn't mind looking at the White House from afar, but don't expect me to sit up at his table. I'm sure I'd spill something right down the front of my dress or else embarrass you in some other way. I'm just Tuatha'an, a plain old tinker's daughter, Reed, not a fancied up Southern belle or even a Yankee."

"So you can put the Yankee and the Southern belle in the same sentence now, can you?" Reed asked.

"Don't test my mettle," she pointed her fork at him.

He chuckled. He'd already tested her mettle several times. They'd argued. They'd stood together in the middle of a riot. They'd worked together to bring Angelina into the world. Yes, her mettle had been tested and she'd even passed the testing process. She'd stood beside him when she thought he was just a Yankee soldier going home after the war, and still yet didn't seem to give rat's fanny if he was rich or poor.

Sometime late that night, Geneva awoke from sleep in a sweat born from pure fear. She'd been dreaming again. The deputy had a long knife and this time Geneva was beneath the sheets, not a jelly-encrusted dress form. She sat straight up in her bed, checked to make sure the baby was all right and then looked over at Reed, but he wasn't in his bed.

"Reed!" She came off the bed in one jump. She met him in the middle of the car, running into his chest so hard she bounced backward.

"I'm right here. I've got you," he wrapped his arms around her and drew her into his embrace.

"I was dreaming he was there again and this time it was me under the sheets and then I woke up and you were gone and I was afraid he was back," she blurted without raising her head, suddenly realizing her face was buried in a soft nest of curly hair on a broad muscular chest.

"It's all right," he rubbed her back.

His touch penetrated the sheer lawn fabric of her nightrail and scorched her skin.

She raised her face to look into his eyes. Even in the moonlight pouring in from the window, she could see the warmth in them. At least for a few seconds. Then they slowly closed, leaving nothing but heavy black lashes feathered out across his cheeks as he sought her lips.

The kiss weakened her legs even more than the first

two had done. She leaned into it, nipping his lower lip with her teeth as she groaned. The world stood still; the train moved faster; there was humming somewhere near the ceiling; her heart raced; her soul sighed.

"Reed," she whispered when he broke away and gathered her back into his arms again. "What are we going to do about us?"

"Did that affect you the same way it did me?" he whispered.

"I don't know about you, but the first time you kissed me, I thought I'd faint from wanting you. It wasn't right though. I'm a widow. You don't want a plain tinker's daughter. You are important and rich. I'm just Geneva. The second time you kissed me I hated you for making me feel again. I wanted to be numb the rest of my life. I wanted to raise my daughter and never look at another man," she said honestly, still leaning into his bare chest.

"And now?" he asked.

"Now I don't want to live my life without you. I don't want you to go away and I'm scared. You've got family in Love's Valley. You've got friends. What would they think if you brought home a woman like me? I'm too tall. You yourself thought I was fat. I . . ." she paused.

"Shhh," he tilted her chin up and put his finger on her mouth. "You are tall. But I'm taller. And what was fat is lying on that bed—a gorgeous baby girl. You're beautiful, Geneva. And I've fallen in love with you. And yes, ma'am, it will cause a stink at the Hamilton household. Because you see, I gave my sister two promises in a letter just before I left Savannah and got on the stage with you. I promised I would come home a bachelor and not bring home a Southern wife like my brothers, and I promised I'd be there for her wedding. I guess she'll have to forgive one of the promises."

"Which one?" Geneva asked.

"The one about not coming home married to a Southern woman. That is if you'll have this Yankee for your husband?" he asked.

"Is that a proposal?" she asked.

"It is. We can get married in Washington and then go on home to Love's Valley if that would suit you. I know you're supposed to be in widow's weeds a whole year, but your circumstances aren't normal so why should you follow standard procedure?" He tilted her chin back again and treated himself to another delicious kiss. If all kisses affected him this way, he'd get precious little work done in Love's Valley this fall.

"Are you sure?" She forced her mouth from his.

"I've never been surer of anything in my entire life," he told her. "Indigo will be a spoiled brat of a young woman. But that's the way she's always been. I've got a feeling you and Adelida will get along fine. And Momma will love you."

"Then the answer is yes," she said. "But I want a priest, a Catholic church, and I want to go to confession before we're married. I want to know for sure that the church recognizes our marriage. If the father says we must wait until the mourning time is over, then I want to respect that. I don't want to ever feel like I'm living in sin again."

"Agreed," he sealed his promise with another kiss.

Chapter Seventeen

"Bless me Father, for I have sinned," Geneva whispered so low in the darkened room that the priest had to strain to hear her. Then she went into a list of her sins beginning from the last time she'd been to confessional, which was two years before. Back when she was still an innocent young woman.

On the front pew of the church, Reed stretched Angelina out on his knees. It was evident she knew his voice as he told her all about Love's Valley and how she'd have a pony of her own as soon as she could walk. "But first we have to ride the train again to Harrisburg. We'll have our own car and you can wallow on the bed as much as you like," he whispered. What could be taking Geneva so long? After he'd heard their confessions, what would be the priest's opinion on a marriage between them? Reed would wait a year if that was the decision. It would go fast if he could see Geneva and Angelina often. Maybe Douglass and Monroe would even offer to let her live in a room of their big new home and she'd be right there in Love's Valley.

Geneva's face was shiny with tears when she joined him on the front pew. He brushed kisses across her cheeks and eyelids, but didn't touch her lips. Not until he heard the verdict. Not until after he'd been absolved of his sins, and they were many. He hadn't been inside a confessional since the week before he went to war. He had committed so many sins since then he scarcely knew where to begin. He laid Angelina in Geneva's arms and went into the familiar little room.

"I have sinned, Father, and I'm not sure I deserve a blessing or forgiveness," he said softly.

Geneva looked into her daughter's eyes. She'd told the father about the night she'd prayed the baby would be born dead. That may have been her worst sin yet, and the father had told her that God was forgiving and loving and understood the anguish she felt. She'd hate to face the future without Angelina or Reed either. She asked herself difficult questions as she sat on the front pew, surrounded by all the peaceful things she loved. The first one: *How can I really love Reed in such a short time?* The answer came quickly from her heart. *Because you can trust him to keep his word and he makes you feel special.* The second one: *Why did I have to suffer the past year? Why couldn't I have just met Reed and fallen in love with him without having to go through the torment of Hiriam and the disappointment in my father?* The memory of her mother's soft

Southern voice answered her so close to her ear she could practically feel the warmth of her breath. *What you have been through makes you the woman you are today, the one Reed fell in love with.* The third one: *How will I survive a whole year so close to him and yet so far away?* The memory of her father's voice from far away answered that one. *That which does not kill us makes us stronger.*

The door to the confessional opened and Reed's presence filled the room. His mother had always said that confession is good for the soul. For the first time in his life, he understood what she was talking about. He sat down beside Geneva and waited patiently for the priest. He threw his arm around her, drawing her close to his side, enjoying the way she fit, not only physically but spiritually. How could he have ever thought she was a fat, dirty woman? If he'd looked a little closer he would have seen the beauty under the soot and would have realized the only thing fat about her was her middle where Angelina waited.

"Hmmmm," the priest was right in front of them and neither one had heard him arrive.

Geneva looked up with a bright smile. Peace, for the first time in years, filled her whole being.

"I've given your plight some serious thought. The war hasn't changed the church's views, yet . . ." he paused.

"We came with the agreement that we would abide by whatever God says is best for our lives," Geneva said softly. "I do not want to feel like I'm living in sin again. I want the blessing of the Church."

"Are you really ready to marry this man, Geneva?" the priest asked. "Do you need time to heal your body and soul from the sins committed against you?"

"I'm ready to marry Reed today, tomorrow, next week, next year. I've fallen in love with him, and I finally realized while I was sitting here why things have happened the way they have. The experiences I've survived have made me the woman I am today. Made me the woman Reed fell in love with. And what he's endured has made him the man he is today, the man I fell in love with. I'll marry him whenever it's right. That's your decision, Father. Is it right today?" she asked.

"And you Reed? You're taking on a widow with a child. Are you sure that in a year or five years you won't regret your decision?" the priest asked.

"Father, I love Geneva and that love has grown from a friendship born in difficulties. I didn't set out to love her. Matter of fact, I fought against it even when my heart said it wasn't having anyone else. But love alone won't carry us from today through the last breath of life. So I have to admit that I also respect her. She's a strong woman, one who will be an honor to ride the river of life with. One who won't jump ship midway down the journey from here to eternity. I believe that with my whole heart. Love takes us through some tough times and unites us as one, but respect will keep us going if ever love gets thin. I'm not a boy. I've been to through the ravages of war. I'll wait for her until it's proper so she'll be happy, but I'll still feel the same next week or in a year. I love and respect this woman and I want her to be my partner for life," Reed said.

Tears welled up in Geneva's eyes. She wished she had his words on paper so that she could read them every day. No matter what vows were read on their wedding day, she'd always remember what he said sitting on the front pew of a Catholic church in Washington D. C. His words about making her a partner seared into her heart like a burning brand. Not a slave to do his bidding. Not someone to walk on and treat like dirt, but a partner. No matter what she came from or had been, she'd be his partner.

"In any other circumstance I would advise you both to wait. It would be my thought that you needed more time to live in normal situations. What you've experienced together has been extraordinary. Any one of those traumatic experiences would mark your judgment. However, I think you have both come out on the other side of those experiences more mature because of the other one. I see in your lives what I wish I could see in every couple who comes to ask me to perform the marriage ceremony. I see honesty, love, and most importantly, I see respect. So yes, today I will marry you and I will also, as Reed has asked, christen this baby," he said.

"Right now?" Geneva gasped.

"If you are truly ready. I will change my robes and prepare the service with a complete mass so you can partake together of the Holy Communion," he said.

"Forgive me, Reed, for saying it like that but I'm ready. I was just wondering if I was dressed properly for a real wedding," she said.

"You are beautiful," Reed took her hand and looked deeply into those blue eyes that absolutely mesmerized him. "In that old dress you wore before Angelina was born, you were beautiful. In the traveling suit, you were beautiful. But this is my favorite of all the things you wear, because it's the same color as your eyes."

The priest chuckled. If Harry Reed Hamilton kept that slick silver-coated tongue, there'd be a lot more of the love element to their relationship. "Then I shall change and return in a few minutes," he disappeared into a side room where his robes hung.

An hour later they were officially Mr. and Mrs. Harry Reed Hamilton.

An elderly woman who'd come to light a candle for her husband that morning, and the middle-aged man who'd been weeding the flower bed in the church courtyard, served as witnesses to the wedding, signing their names on the license which the priest said he would file at the Washington courthouse the next day.

"And now," he paused before he completed the last empty space. "The date?"

"Today is July twenty-ninth, isn't it?" Geneva said.

"But what year?" the priest asked.

A grin spreading across Reed's face as he realized the concession the priest was making in even offering such a thing. It would make Angelina his daughter in reality as well as in his heart.

The priest smiled. "I'm just simply asking you to

tell me what the year is. I can't seem to remember without a calendar in front of me."

Geneva chewed the inside of her lip. Would it be a sin? Would she worry forever that her child would find out the truth and hate her for it? Yet, would it make Angelina feel left out when other children came, and they would. Geneva wanted a yard full of kids, running and playing, fighting and loving, standing up for each other.

"Geneva?" Reed asked.

"On this one, I need to know if you are really, really sure, Reed. It would be closing the books to ever telling her the truth about Hiriam," she said.

"Redemption is blotting out the past so the heart can be opened for a sweet future, remember? Angelina is my daughter. I brought her into this world. I saved her from the wild hog. I miss her when I have to be away from her. She's my firstborn, not born of my blood, no, but born of my heart. If the father will be kind enough to register our marriage at one year ago today, then write her christening date and birth in as this year, I would be glad to blot out the past and make her mine in every sense of the word."

"Then the past is blotted out," Geneva said.

"Done," the priest wrote the date on the paper. "We shall christen this baby now. Her name is Angelina? What is her middle name and what is her christening name?"

"Reed?" Geneva asked.

"That's up to you," he said.

"No, sir, we are a partnership. I'll give her a middle

name. Been thinkin' about it for a while now. But you are to decide her christening name," Geneva said.

"All right, then, her christening name shall be Virginia. Because it was in Lynchburg that I came to terms with my own heart and admitted to myself that I'd truly fallen in love with you and that I did not want to fall out of love with you. That I never did. So her name is Virginia to remind me always of that time," Reed said.

"And her middle name is Harryette. Spelled H-A-R-R-Y-E-T-T-E, please, Father. That way she is named for her father, Harry Reed Hamilton. We'll save the name Reed for our first son," Geneva said, high color filling her cheeks and making her freckles even more prominent.

"Then Angelina Harryette Virginia Hamilton, it is," Father Michael smiled down on the baby and began the ceremony.

They boarded their own private train car in the middle of the morning. Destination: Harrisburg, Pennsylvania. The walls were covered in navy blue silk. Two beds occupied one end, along with two easy chairs. Newspapers on the table between them. Reed had ordered lunch to be brought at noon, a mid-afternoon snack at three, and dinner at six.

Geneva laid Angelina down on one of the beds and turned to face her new husband in their honeymoon train car. She wound her arms around his neck and pulled his lips down to hers. Yes, it was still there. That warm, mushy feeling in the pits of her stomach that wanted more than a kiss.

"It's two hours until they bring lunch," she murmured softly in his ear.

"But it's broad daylight," Reed chuckled.

"And Angelina is asleep in her bed. This is our bed, Reed Hamilton," she pointed at the empty four-poster beckoning to them both.

"I love you, Geneva," he said simply.

"And I love you, Reed," she said.

Angelina Harryette Virginia Hamilton slept until noon.

Chapter Eighteen

Geneva literally gasped when the hack Reed had hired in the little town of Shirleysburg, Pennsylvania, reached Love's Valley, but when it turned down the lane toward the house, she was breathless. The house loomed, big, sturdy, and ominous in the bright afternoon sunlight. Red brick with two white pillars gleaming against all that dark brick. Roses climbed up the porch posts and the flowerbeds were abundant with riotous color. Reed had promised her that they'd build in the valley between what he called the Blacklog and Shade Mountains, but she'd never expected anything to be so lovely. Her mind reached ahead into the future and began to plan a house, a white one, so big it could hold a huge growing family. One as breathtakingly beautiful as the one she stood in awe of at that time. One where her sons could bring their wives home and she'd meet them on the front porch.

Who was she kidding? How would a mere tinker's daughter fit in among people who'd lived like this their whole lives? A shiver of fear tried to prickle the hair on her arms but she shook it away. The past was gone and yes, she'd been a tinker's daughter and Hiriam Garner's wife, both, but today she was Mrs. Reed Hamilton and she wouldn't dishonor him by being a shrinking violet. She'd stand tall and be proud of who she was.

"Don't be afraid," Reed drew her closer to his side, reading her mind. "They won't bite. All but Indigo that is. She might bare her fangs at first, but she'll love you by morning."

"I'm not afraid. I'm glad to be here with you. It's been a glorious week and Reed, I've wished I'd never have to share you," she said honestly.

"You don't. I'm yours forever, but family is a good thing, Geneva. It means Angelina will have cousins and it means you'll have sisters and brothers," he assured her.

A tiny wisp of a woman sat on the front porch swing holding a baby in her lap. Her jet black hair was pulled back in a bun at the nape of her neck and a few wrinkles creased her cheeks.

"Your mother?" Geneva asked when the cab stopped and Reed hopped out first, and then helped her and Angelina out.

"No, I don't know who she is. My first guess would

be Douglass' mother, but no one mentioned that she was coming," he said.

"Hello," the lady said with a definite Texas twang. "I bet you are Reed. They've been talking about you coming any day now and Indigo has been fretting. I'm Douglass' mother. I couldn't let my first grandchild be born without me."

"Yes, I'm Reed. Where is everyone? Is that Monroe and Douglass' baby then?" He paid the driver who'd already unloaded three trunks and turned the rig around to go back to town.

"Reed!" Indigo bounded out the door and wrapped her arms tightly around his neck. "You're home. You made it in time for the wedding. You kept your promises."

"Harry Reed." His mother wiped her hands on her apron tail as she appeared behind her daughter, crossed the porch and pushed Indigo away for her own hugs.

"Hey, brother," Monroe pulled Douglass behind him by the hand. "We've been waiting for you."

"Reed," Adelida yelled from the upstairs window. "We're on our way down right now. You save a hug for me."

"Who is this?" Indigo asked bluntly at the same time Rueben and Adelida reached the porch.

"Everyone is here, now, I guess," Reed looked around at the family, felt the love surrounding him as well as the heat from Indigo's eyes.

"Yes, all but Ellie and Colum and they're up overseeing the building of their new house . . . . And who is this?" she asked again, narrowing her eyes to stare at Geneva. Lord almighty, the woman was almost as tall as Reed, and she was holding a baby in her arms.

"I have a surprise. This is my wife, Geneva, and this is our daughter, born July first, Angelina Harryette Virginia Hamilton," he said proudly, pulling Geneva to his side. "I'm sure you will forgive me for breaking one of my promises, Indigo. But I couldn't tell you and expect you to keep a secret like that. So I crossed my fingers behind my back when I made it. Geneva is one of the Tuatha'an, the traveling people, or tinkers as we know them. She was raised in the South but I met her in Savannah."

"Well, you old rat. You never even let on when we saw you at the beginning of the summer," Adelida said. "Welcome to the Hamilton family, Geneva. And let's see that baby. A girl, and she looks exactly like you. Thank goodness. Reed might be handsome like all these Hamilton men, sugar, but no one would want a baby girl to look like him. However I do believe she has his chin," Adelida took the baby from Geneva and held her out for everyone to look at.

"I beat you by three days," Monroe laughed. "Michael Milford Luke Hamilton, born June twenty-eighth. We call him Ford. So what do you call your daughter? I hope not Harryette. Remember our first grade school teacher? She had a mole on her lip. Looks like we'll raise our kids together."

"Looks like it and we call her Angelina. And I'd forgotten all about Miss Harriett. We spelled the name different than the mole lipped lady, though. Our daughter's name is H-A-R-R-Y-E-T-T-E," Reed said. "That way she's named after me. Now Momma has a granddaughter as well as a grandson to keep her young."

"I don't like this one bit," Indigo said, her dark blue eyes flashing anger, her tall stance leaving no doubt she was about to have a first-rate temper fit. "Of all the brothers, I expected you to have the most sense. I didn't expect you to come dragging home a Southern woman, much less a tinker's daughter. Don't you have any pride, Reed Hamilton? These other two and Ellie, too, haven't shown a lick of sense but you've stooped the lowest of any of them."

"Indigo!" Laura Hamilton exclaimed.

"I'm old enough to speak my mind and I don't care what any of you say, I'm going to do it," she said.

Geneva took one step forward and slapped Indigo on the cheek. "Miss Hamilton. I would not presume upon the right to call you Indigo even if we are sisters by marriage now, since it appears you are going to despise me so much. However, let it be known right now that even though you may hate me because of the fact that I come from a family of plain old tinkers, you will not talk about my husband like that. He's the most wonderful person on the face of this green earth. Now you owe him an apology. Whether you give it or not marks whether you are an adult or a child."

Quietness prevailed. A rose petal falling to the ground would have made enough noise to deafen the whole crowd.

"Momma, are you going to let her talk to me like that?" Indigo held her red cheek.

"I think she has the right to talk to you like that," Laura said. "And I think you got off easy. If anyone would have slandered your father like you just did your brother, I would have snatched them baldheaded. I'd hate to see you in that lovely veil next week without any hair."

"I'm sorry Reed," Indigo said petulantly. "I don't like all this but I'll learn to live with it"

"Thank you Indigo," he bit the inside of his lip to keep from howling with laughter. So his sassy sister had met her match in his new wife, and he couldn't even laugh. Later, he kept telling himself, he'd go to the bunkhouse and roar until tears rolled down his cheeks.

"I suppose on that note, we'd better all go inside and make some cold lemonade to cool down some tempers," Douglass said, biting her own lip. This new bride of Reed's would fit right in with the other Southern wives and Douglass for one couldn't wait to get to know her better. "And Adelida, I think you've looked enough pretty off that baby girl. It's my turn to hold her. Come on in, Geneva, you can squeeze some lemons while I see if holding a little girl is as much fun as holding a son. Oh, here come Ellie and Colum. Momma, get Colum acquainted with Reed and tell Ellie we're making lemonade in the kitchen and there's a baby girl for her to meet. She'll tear up the house getting there. She wants a daughter so badly she can taste it."

"Welcome home," Reed kissed Geneva passionately on the mouth in front of the whole family. "I love you," he whispered softly.

"I love you and this place too," she said loudly. "I want to build my white house with a porch in this valley and I was wondering if Mother Hamilton could give me startings of those red roses?"

"Just call me Momma," Laura hugged Geneva, "Mother Hamilton sounds old, doesn't it? Just Momma will be fine. And those girls better get all the lovin' they want from that granddaughter of mine in the next few minutes, because my turn is next and I'm not letting go of her for a long time."

Geneva smiled brightly and blew a kiss at Reed.

She'd found her place in the world, as Reed's wife, as Angelina's mother, as a daughter in Laura's heart, and as a new bride in Love's Valley, Pennsylvania.

Geneva's past was truly blotted out and her heart had opened for a sweet future.